For Gold or Soul?

The Story of a Great Department Store

by

Lurana Sheldon

Double9 BOOKS

For Gold or Soul?
The Story of a Great Department Store
by Lurana Sheldon

ISBN: 978-93-61420-29-0

Published by

DOUBLE 9 BOOKS
2/13-B, Ansari Road
Daryaganj, New Delhi – 110002
info@double9books.com
www.double9books.com
Tel. 011-40042856

ABOUT THE AUTHOR

Lurana W. Sheldon was an American novelist, poet, and short story writer who also served as a newspaper editor. Her published work totaled almost one million words. She claimed to have made a living in fifteen distinct and completely unrelated businesses, including bookkeeping, company management, journalism, working in a chemical laboratory, purchasing dry goods, and composing stories. She was a suffrage campaigner who opposed prohibition. Sheldon was the first poet in the United States to utilize her abilities to promote birth control. Sheldon's poetry appeared on the editorial page of The New York Times so frequently that her name became synonymous with the publication. Sheldon gained sociological information through his medical education and extensive study of the underprivileged. One of her accomplishments was a sociological lecture in verse called "The Alien," which was given in New York and internationally in 1915. One poem from this lecture, "The Night Court," was widely read and reproduced. Sheldon wrote many novels and serial stories, as well as many short stories and special pieces, and over a thousand poems, which appeared in practically every major magazine and newspaper in the United States. For many years, she also composed a great quantity of unsigned verses.

CONTENTS

CHAPTER I
IN THE SUPERINTENDENT'S OFFICE

The monster department store of Messrs. Denton, Day & Co. was thronged with shoppers, although the morning was still young.

Scores of pale-faced women and narrow-chested men stood behind the counters, while "cash girls," with waxen cheeks and scrawny figures, darted here and there on their ceaseless errands. On the fifth floor of the building, where the firm's offices were quartered, a score or more of anxious girls and women waited eagerly for an opportunity to enter their applications for service.

At last a private door was opened by an elfish-looking boy, and the earliest applicant was allowed to enter, the boy warning her, as she did so, to "be quick about it."

"So you are looking for work? Well, what can you do? Got any references? Talk fast, for I have no time to waste on applicants."

The speaker was Mr. Duncan Forbes, junior partner, as well as business superintendent of the establishment, and the person spoken to was a beautiful girl, about seventeen years of age, who had called to apply for a position as saleswoman.

"I have never worked before, sir," said the young girl, trying to obey and talk as rapidly as possible, "but I am sure I could learn in a very short time, if only you will give me a trial as saleswoman. Do please give me a trial!"

The keen-eyed superintendent looked over her scrutinizingly.

He at once saw that she was a girl unaccustomed to drudgery, and that her clothes were of fine materials, although they were fast growing shabby.

Her cheeks were rosy from plenty of exercise in the sun and air, her figure was rounded, and her carriage graceful.

She did not resemble in the least the sallow-faced specimens of womanhood who swarmed over Denton, Day & Co.'s various departments, but these very differences seemed to influence him against her. He wanted girls with experience, and experience, in their line of business, meant haggard expressions and sallow faces.

His answer was as heartless as crisp words could make it.

"Can't do it! The thing would be ridiculous! We have no time nor inclination to break in green hands, besides, we've got help enough at present; it's almost our dull season."

"But I would be a cash girl, anything!" the girl urged, eagerly. "Oh, I need work so badly, and I've been all over the city!"

The tears had risen to her eyes and were trembling on her lashes. She clasped her hands entreatingly as the superintendent rudely turned his back upon her.

"Can't do it, I tell you, so there's no use taking up any more of my time! Well, what is it, Watkins?"

The question was addressed to an employee, a pale, slim young man, who had just entered the office.

"Excuse me, Mr. Forbes, but there's three clerks absent to-day. They have sent word that they are sick. Mr. Gibson told me to tell you."

"Who are they, do you know?"

Mr. Forbes spoke sharply, his face flushing with anger.

"Miss Jennings and Miss Brown—" began the young man, but his superior stopped him before he could finish.

"That Miss Jennings is faking! She is no more sick than I am! This is the third time this month that she has staid away because of sickness! It's probably an excuse to go on some picnic or other. Tell Mr. Gibson that I say to fine her double the regular amount. We must put a stop to this sham sickness among the women clerks; it's getting too frequent!"

"But I am sure Miss Jennings is sick," began Mr. Watkins, impetuously. "You should hear her cough! And I know her mother died of consumption."

"You know too much for your own good, Watkins," broke in the superintendent, sharply. "Just keep your knowledge to yourself if you wish to hold your position in this establishment!"

A flush rose quickly to the young man's brow. He bit his lips and locked his fingers together nervously.

It was plain that another word would have meant his immediate discharge, and there was an invalid mother depending upon him. He was obliged to hold his peace, though the words almost choked him. "Then I am to tell Mr. Gibson to double Miss Jennings' fine."

The superintendent broke in upon him again in his snappiest manner.

He had suddenly turned and caught sight of the timid young applicant, who was standing almost motionless in the centre of the office.

"No!" he roared out, angrily. "Tell him to discharge Miss Jennings at once! Here is a girl he can take on in her place. She's green, but Miss Fairbanks, the buyer, can train her."

"Oh! no, sir! Not for the world!"

It was a cry of almost horror that issued from the young girl's lips. Even Mr. Forbes looked startled, and he was not usually startled at anything.

The applicant was standing before him now, with her head held high and her blue eyes flashed like diamonds over his shameful proposition.

"Oh, no, sir! I beg that you will not dream of doing such a thing. I would starve before I would deprive that poor girl of her position. If you have no place for me, I will go at once. If I were to take her place it would be a cruel injustice!"

She looked him fearlessly in the face as she spoke the words. Her whole manner had changed. She was timid no longer.

Mr. Forbes stared at her curiously for half a minute. He saw that there was a spirit in her that would make her valuable in business.

In an instant his manner changed to a studied indifference. He rubbed his hands together gently, toying with a fine ring upon his finger.

"But I shall discharge Miss Jennings any way, so if you do not accept the position I will give it to some one else," he said. "You can take it or leave it. Decide quick; which is it?"

For the space of a second the applicant wavered, but in that second she read something in Mr. Watkins' expression. His look was unmistakable. He was waiting to see if she faltered in her decision.

She raised her head and looked Mr. Forbes squarely in the eyes.

"I thank you, sir, for your offer," she said, as calmly as she could, "but I would rather die than do anything I considered wrong, and this act of yours is both wicked and unjust! God will punish you for your cruelty to that poor Miss Jennings!"

She turned and walked toward the door, leaving Mr. Forbes and Mr. Watkins both staring after her.

CHAPTER II
A HUMBLE BEGINNING

It was the second time that the young girl had succeeded in startling the superintendent, but this time she had accomplished far more than she knew, for her few words fell upon the brain of the business man with a significance that for a moment almost overcame him. Under favorable conditions far less thrilling words than these have taken root and yielded a bountiful harvest, but the time for this man's awakening was at hand. His only son, a youth of nineteen, was lying critically ill at home, and, while Mr. Forbes was worldly, he was also unusually superstitious, and her words, "God will punish you," rang in his ears like a blast from a trumpet.

Almost involuntarily he took a step forward. He could not explain so unusual an action.

"Wait!" he said, peremptorily.

The young girl paused, with her hand on the door.

"I am not so cruel as you think, miss," he said, trying to speak as sternly as ever, "so your speech just now was entirely uncalled for. If you are really in desperate need of work, I can give you a position as packer at three dollars a week. This is the best I can offer. Do you care to accept it?"

"I will take any position where I am not defrauding any one else, sir," the girl answered, quickly. "But I could not accept what belongs to another. I think that money so earned would prove a curse instead of a blessing."

The superintendent stared at her with a puzzled look.

"What is your name?" he asked, after this second scrutiny of her features.

"Faith Marvin, sir," replied the applicant, promptly.

Mr. Forbes repeated the name a little absently.

Miss Marvin watched him eagerly. Her face had flushed a little.

"I've heard that name somewhere, but I can't think where," remarked Mr. Forbes, with a glance toward Mr. Watkins, "but it don't matter about the name. Come to-morrow morning at seven-thirty, sharp, and I'll set you to work. Well, what is it, Jackson?"

Another employee had entered hurriedly.

As he stood directly in her way, Miss Marvin could not leave the office at once, so she was forced to hear the conversation that followed.

"There's one of them Government Inspectors on the first floor, sir," reported the newcomer, "and she's a sharp one, I can tell you! Mr. Gibson wants to know if you'll come down and see her. It's the lavatories, sir; she's determined to see 'em."

The change that came over the superintendent's face at this announcement was astonishing. His naturally florid features grew as red as a blaze, and he actually increased in size as he swelled with indignation.

"Another of those prying, inquisitive people, hey!" he cried furiously. "Another spy to look over the store and report to the Board of Health that our plumbing is out of order! Tell Mr. Gibson I'll come down at once, and see here, Jackson, tell him to keep her on the first floor. I'll send the porter to the basement to open the windows. They shall not get ahead of me, the impudent creatures. The firm of Denton, Day & Co. is not going to waste money on new-fangled sanitary improvements just to please a lot of cranks with sensitive noses!"

Mr. Jackson hurried away at once to report to the manager, Mr. Gibson, leaving his employer still fuming and growing angrier every minute.

He was so terrible in his anger that Miss Marvin was glad when she was able to slip through the door at last and pick her way through the group of applicants, who were still patiently waiting.

Mr. Forbes took no notice of her departure, as he was pushing back the papers on his desk, preparatory to closing it.

Suddenly he uttered an exclamation that made Mr. Watkins jump. He had been looking over a file of letters, but turned quickly to see what was the matter.

"Quick, Watkins, stop her! Stop her!" cried the superintendent, sharply. "There were five hundred dollars on my desk ten minutes ago! It's gone, every cent of it. Quick, I tell you. Stop her!"

"Stop who?"

Mr. Watkins was over to the door before he asked the question.

"Faith Marvin, that girl that was looking for a job. The money was on the desk while she was here in the office. She's stolen it and gone, and to think, I offered her a position!"

Mr. Forbes ran his hands through his hair and glared at Mr. Watkins.

"Well, why don't you go?" he thundered, as the young man stood stock still, staring at him like a dummy.

Mr. Watkins hurried from the office on his disagreeable errand. He would have staked his all that the girl had not touched the money.

Mr. Forbes made a hurried search through his desk while the young man was gone. He was so upset about his loss that he had forgotten the Government Inspector completely.

The five hundred dollars was not to be found and Mr. Forbes was allowing his temper full vent—through the usual medium of blasphemous profanity.

He was so positive that the girl would be caught at once that he almost gasped when Mr. Watkins came back without her.

"She's gone, sir," said the young man, shortly. "The detective here saw her go out. She went down the elevator and out the side entrance. Bob's description of her is all right. I am sure it was Miss Marvin."

Bob Hardy, a store detective, came in while Mr. Watkins was speaking.

"I'm right, sir; couldn't be mistaken. She was out like an arrow," he said, respectfully.

"And to think that I was stupid enough not to take her address, but probably she would have lied about it. Those creatures are always tricky," snarled the superintendent.

The detective took a step forward and removed his hat.

"There'll be no trouble in finding her, sir," he said; "I know who she is. I've seen her a dozen times before, and I'm not apt to be mistaken."

The superintendent looked at him questioningly, so the officer went on:

"She's the daughter of Douglass Marvin, who used to keep a bookstore in this block. Denton, Day & Co. put him out of business when they opened their book department. He committed suicide soon after he failed. He left a wife and this daughter, and not a penny."

"Then the deed was deliberate!" cried Mr. Forbes, almost choking with anger. "The girl is trying to square accounts for what we did to her father!"

"Nonsense!"

Mr. Watkins uttered the word with extraordinary daring.

"She came here to look for a job, and you have offered her one, Mr. Forbes! Mark my words, she'll be on hand to-morrow morning at half-past seven!"

"And the money?"

The superintendent turned upon the speaker with a perfect thundercloud darkening his face.

"Perhaps, as you know so much, Watkins, you can explain about the money!"

Before any one could answer the door opened and Mr. Jackson came in again.

"Please, Mr. Forbes, the manager says come down quick, sir!" he cried, with a grin. "He can't keep that Government woman out of the basement much longer."

CHAPTER III
A GLIMPSE OF THE DARKNESS

When Faith Marvin reached the employees' entrance of Denton, Day & Co.'s department store the next morning at half-past seven, she was shown into a room that was a sort of cloak-room, lunch-room and lavatory combined, in the basement of the building.

The place was poorly lighted and badly ventilated, and there were fully two hundred women and girls crowding and jostling each other while they hung up their wraps and put on false sleeves and black aprons.

For a while the din was confusing, but Faith soon began to see and hear distinctly.

She was amazed and then horrified at the snatches of conversation she heard. Even a little cash girl used language that was almost profanity, and others made remarks of a most heartless nature.

Here and there Faith saw a face that looked different from the rest. They were mostly pale, pinched faces, bearing deep lines of care, but they all looked stolid, hardened and indifferent.

"I suppose it's the hard work and worry," whispered Faith, involuntarily. Just then she felt some one tapping her smartly on the shoulder.

She turned quickly and confronted a woman about her own height, who had the sharpest pair of eyes that Faith ever remembered seeing.

"Is this Faith Marvin?"

The woman spoke softly, but her voice was cold and metallic.

"It is," answered Faith. "I was told to come this morning. Can you give me any information as to where I am to go? I see the others are all hurrying upstairs, but there is no one to direct me."

The woman had not taken her eyes from Faith's face while the young girl was talking. She seemed to be scanning her features with more than ordinary curiosity.

"Where do you live?"

The question was asked by the woman in a business-like manner, but as Faith hesitated before answering the sharp eyes twinkled a little.

"Am I obliged to give my address?" asked Faith very slowly.

"Certainly—it's the rule of the house."

The woman frowned as she answered.

Faith gave her address in a faltering voice. She had hoped to be able to keep that a secret.

The woman wrote down the address on a piece of paper.

"A mother and father?" was the next brief question.

Faith's face was scarlet now, but she answered promptly.

"A mother, yes; but my father is dead. He was Douglass Marvin. He owned a bookstore in this block. When Denton, Day & Co. opened their book department my father was ruined."

The woman looked at her enviously as she asked the next question.

"How did you happen to come to this store to look for work? Don't you resent the injury that was done to your father?"

In a second Faith Marvin's eyes filled with tears.

"Oh, no!" she cried hastily. "I bear no resentment! I know it is always the weak who must suffer! I came here because I was desperately in need of work. My mother's health is failing and we are penniless."

"Well, it's lucky you're so forgiving," said the woman with a peculiar stare; "but come, you must report to Miss Fairbanks, the buyer in the ribbon department! She's on the first floor. I'll take you to her."

Miss Fairbanks looked Faith over almost as sharply as the other woman had done.

She was short-handed that morning, so there was no time for preliminaries.

"Ever work in a store before?" was her first business-like question.

"No, madam," said Faith timidly; "I have had no experience at all, but I am sure I shall learn quickly if you will be so kind as to teach me."

She was beginning to tremble a little for fear the woman would not try her.

"Oh, I guess you'll do if you are not too stuck up," said the buyer carelessly. "Girls who have never worked in a store always think they know it all, and that sort of thing doesn't go, not in my department!"

She led Faith up to one of the gates at the ribbon counter and showed her how to crawl up to the packer's desk above the shelves, where the stock was kept.

"Now, when one of the saleswomen hands you up a check and some ribbon you must measure the ribbon carefully to see that the firm is not being cheated," she explained in a shrill voice, "and if one of the girls makes a mistake report it to me immediately."

Faith was up by this time and trying to accommodate herself to the awkward position, while she listened intently to all the buyer's instructions.

The packer's desk was so low that it cramped her limbs even in sitting, and Faith soon saw that she was older and larger than any other girl in that position on the floor.

This fact alone made her feel awkward and uncomfortable, and when she saw one of the clerks looking up at her and tittering she blushed and nearly cried through sheer embarrassment. To add to her nervousness she soon noticed that two men, who were standing in one of the aisles, were watching her every movement for some reason or other. She was thankful when the checks and goods began to come up. It was a relief to keep her eyes on the different packages.

Faith had never had much experience in doing up parcels, but she managed very nicely after her hands stopped trembling.

Long before noon she was aching in every muscle. The dust that rose from the floor was irritating her throat and the store was so hot that her head was aching.

She looked down at the clerks, who had been on their feet steadily since eight o'clock, and began to understand the callousness of their expressions. A great throb of pity for them, rather than for herself, dimmed her eyes for an instant so that she could not see her packages.

During that first few hours Faith could not help noticing how often Number 89 sent up goods to be wrapped. There were double as many sales to her credit as to any of the others at the counter, and at a leisure moment she leaned over and looked down at her.

Just as she did so Number 89 was seized with a fit of coughing. It was over in a minute, but was extremely severe while it lasted.

In spite of herself Faith could not resist glancing at her often, and once when she caught her eye she smiled at her pleasantly.

The effect was magical.

Number 89 soon handed up a check and three yards of ribbon, and as their hands met over the goods she caught and squeezed the "packer's" little finger.

"I'm sorry you have such a cough!"

Faith whispered the words quickly.

Number 89 was about to reply when Miss Fairbanks, the buyer, passed the counter.

"No loitering, Miss Jennings! Don't you see there are customers waiting? Forward at once! And you, packer, attend to business! I see you have goods in your hands. Wrap them up this minute!"

CHAPTER IV
SOME UNPLEASANT INFORMATION

Faith's face turned scarlet, but she obeyed at once. The next instant the buyer was forgotten. She was thinking of Miss Jennings.

So the superintendent had not carried out his threat after all. He could not have forgotten it, his anger had been too genuine.

Faith was thankful enough that the poor girl was still at work, although she looked sick enough to be in bed in the care of a doctor.

As Faith looked at her she could see plainly the stamp of death upon her brow. Her cheeks were bloodless and her eyes were sunken.

After eleven o'clock the girls took turns in going to their luncheons. Some repaired to the basement lunch room, while others who could afford it patronized the nearby restaurants.

It was a pleasant surprise to Faith when Miss Jennings joined her in the lunch room. She had a paper bag in her hand, while Faith carried a small basket.

Almost instinctively the two girls drew away from the others. There was a bond of sympathy between them that they could not account for.

"Do tell me your name," whispered Miss Jennings at once. "It does sound so 'shoppy' to be always saying 'packer.'"

She had opened her bag and taken out a cracker. It was evident that there was no time to be wasted in lunching.

"Call me Faith, if you will. I should like to have you so much! I think it will make me feel a little less strange," was the impulsive answer.

"I will if you'll call me Mary," replied Miss Jennings. "I've just been longing to talk to you all the morning, but there's no dodging Miss Fairbanks' eye; it's always upon you."

"Are we not supposed to speak at all?" asked Faith, who was forgetting to eat her luncheon.

"Oh, yes, we can speak, but not if there are customers waiting. But, tell me, how do you happen to be a packer? You are too old for that kind of work, and quite too clever, I'm sure," said Miss Jennings kindly.

Faith told her how difficult it had been to get any position at all, but she did not dream of telling her how closely her name and work had been connected with the matter.

When she spoke of Mr. Forbes, Miss Jennings fairly shuddered.

"He's a terrible brute," she said in a nervous whisper. "And what do you think, Faith; he's a Sunday-school teacher!"

"Oh no, it can't be!"

Faith caught her breath with a shiver.

"I mean, it doesn't seem possible," she added after a minute.

"Yes, he is," reiterated Miss Jennings soberly.

"I used to go to the same church. Now I don't go to any—I have no use for religion!"

She started coughing, and this gave Faith an opportunity to recover from the shock. When the spasm was over she put her arms affectionately over Miss Jennings' shoulder.

"What has turned you against religion, dear?" she asked very softly. "Is it such men as Mr. Forbes, or just the bitterness from misfortune?"

"Both," said Miss Jennings stubbornly and with a little frown on her face.

"If God is good, why is there so much misery? If He is just, why are we subjected to such terrible oppression, and if He is merciful, why doesn't He hear us when we pray to Him to help us bear our burdens?"

There was a ring of defiance in Miss Jennings' tones. As Faith looked at the pinched features her frame became almost convulsed with anguish.

"Oh, I wish I could answer all your questions, dear!" she cried softly, "and I can, I am sure, if you will just lay aside your bitterness! You are holding black glasses to your own eyes, you poor child, but the light will come; you must keep on praying for it!"

"There is no use, Faith. I've prayed until I'm tired. But don't mind me, dear. I'm what they call a pessimist. I look on the dark side of everything, I suppose; but listen, do you hear what that cash girl is saying?"

Faith shook her head. She had heard nothing but her companion's words.

"Jack Forbes is dying! I saw it in the paper. That's why the old bear isn't here to-day, I suppose! It will just serve him right! I'm not a bit sorry!"

Cash girl Number 9 laughed shrilly as she finished her announcement, and in the remarks that followed Faith learned who Jack Forbes was, and that he was a really fine fellow in spite of his gold-loving father.

In a second she understood also why Miss Jennings was still working. No doubt she would be discharged as soon as Mr. Forbes came back to business.

She moved nearer to her companion as this thought flashed through her mind.

Just then a man stuck his head in the lunch room and looked around. When he saw Faith he stared a minute, and then disappeared very suddenly.

"Hello! Wonder who Hardy is after?" cried one of the girls.

"Who was he?" asked Faith in a whisper of Miss Jennings. "I've seen him watching me several times this morning."

Miss Jennings straightened up and looked at her a minute.

"He's one of the house detectives," she said slowly, "and you happen to be a new girl. Don't bother about him, Faith. They are always watching some one."

"Couldn't hold their jobs if they didn't," chimed in a clerk who had overheard her.

"They have to arrest some one regularly about once in so often. I hope some day they'll arrest the wrong person. It would cost old Denton a pretty penny!"

Just then another clerk from the ribbon counter came up and joined them.

"Did you hear about that inspector coming here yesterday, girls? Well, it didn't do any good, for old Forbes fooled her completely! She didn't get a peep at this room or a sniff at these odors. He means to poison us all to death with sewer gas before he's done with us, but perhaps it will be just as pleasant a death as any other."

Faith Marvin looked up at the speaker with an expression of horror in her eyes.

"Do you mean to say that this place is really unhealthy, and that the firm refuses to comply with the law on such matters?"

"I mean to say that Denton, Day & Co. comply with no law whatever except their own sweet will, and that is to overwork, underpay and bulldoze their employees and then kick them out at a minute's notice."

The girl spoke the words with apparent indifference. Only a long-drawn sigh at their conclusion showed the inmost feeling on the subject.

Faith sprang to her feet with flashing eyes.

"Then that accounts for the haggard faces of the girls whom I have seen this morning! Oh, we must do something at once to alter these conditions! Our employers are but men; they must have hearts in their bosoms!"

"You don't know them, Faith."

It was Miss Jennings who spoke. She was trying her best to conquer another fit of coughing.

"Our employers look upon us girls as so many machines, created for the sole purpose of filling their coffers, and it is this God whom you respect who allows them to abuse us! to grind us into the dust because we are helpless!"

The ring of bitterness in her tones appalled all who heard her except Faith, who threw her arms about her tenderly as she answered:

"No, no, Mary! Don't say that! You are mistaken, dear! God is watching over us all with the tenderest love, and from this whirlwind of injustice He will yet reap a harvest of good! I believe it! I know it, and I shall live to see it!"

CHAPTER V
THE FIRST INSULT

As the young girl gave utterance to these words of prophecy her beautiful eyes were luminous with the fire of a noble purpose. She drew her graceful form to its full height and her voice rang out like the peal of a bell, carrying the message of hope to all that heard it.

Before any one could think of answering, two gentlemen suddenly appeared in the doorway of the poorly lighted room.

When the saleswomen and cash girls saw them they almost stopped breathing, for the two men were the two senior members of the firm, who, for some reason or others, were going over the store together.

Both men stared at Faith in open amazement. It was plain that they had overheard her words, and were surprised at such sentiments from the lips of a greenhorn "packer."

Mr. Denton, a gray-haired man with a fairly benevolent face, seemed more disturbed than his partner over the extraordinary utterance, but as neither of them had heard what Miss Jennings had said, their surprise passed quickly and they began talking together.

"This is the room that they complain of," said Mr. Day, with a contemptuous gesture. "Those sneaking inspectors seem bent on making us as much trouble and expense as possible."

Mr. Denton peered around the room, and even sniffed a little.

"I do not consider it exactly healthy down here," he said, slowly, "but of course you know best, Mr. Day; you have charge of that department. I should not dream of interfering. I know you will do your duty."

"Certainly, certainly," said Mr. Day, promptly. He was a short, stout man, and exceedingly curt and pompous.

"I consider it quite healthy enough for our purpose, Mr. Denton; for what do our salespeople know of modern sanitary improvements?"

"That is so," replied Mr. Denton, with a smile of satisfaction. "What do they know, indeed? Why, they are nearly all of them from the garrets of some tenement or other. They have never been accustomed to anything better, nor perhaps half as comfortable."

They passed out of the room, leaving Faith almost speechless with horror.

In her whole life she had never dreamed of such cowardly injustice.

"Now you know that I am right, Faith," Miss Jennings remarked, with a harsh laugh. "Now you have seen for yourself what we have to expect from our employers."

"They look on us as a lot of rats from some garret or other," added the clerk who had spoken so bitterly before. "But, time's up; we must go back and take in some more money for the darlings."

Faith stifled a sob as she took Miss Jennings' arm and started upstairs. She was pained and disgusted, but by no means discouraged.

"There must be some way," she whispered to Miss Jennings. "It looks very dark, I am willing to admit, but with God all things are possible. I shall not give up. There must be some way of bringing the light into this place. Just now it seems lost in a terrible darkness."

"If God had wished it to be different He would have changed it long ago," muttered Miss Jennings. "But He doesn't care, Faith. Don't tell me that He cares! Why, I am dying, dying, yet He cares nothing about it!"

She broke out into such a terrible fit of coughing that she had to stop on the stairs. Faith kept her arm about her until the spell was over.

When they reached the floor they were two minutes late.

Miss Fairbanks met them and scolded them both severely.

Faith noticed that Miss Jennings did not offer to explain the delay. She would have explained it herself if her companion had not stopped her in a whisper.

"It's no use, Faith; she won't believe it, or, if she did, she'd say I had no right to cough. Poor devil! She treats the people under her just as Forbes treats her. They are a lot of slave drivers and slaves together!"

Faith crawled up to her desk feeling sick at heart. She was overwhelmed with the knowledge of evil which was being forced upon her.

During the afternoon she found time to write a few words on a bit of paper and slip it into Miss Jennings' hand without the buyer seeing her.

"Dear Mary," she wrote, "don't give up in despair. I am sure that Mr. Denton is a good man, only weak and indifferent. I shall pray to-night that

God will open his eyes—then to-morrow I shall try personally to talk to him, for I believe that prayer and effort should always go together. Who knows but that I may be able to brighten things a little? It certainly is worth trying for—to bring the light into dark places."

Miss Jennings watched her chance and handed back her reply.

"It's no use, I tell you, Faith. His heart is like stone. You'll only lose your place. Take my advice and don't do it."

Faith smiled at her brightly as she read the words. They were characteristic of Miss Jennings, philosophic but bitter.

A few minutes later a dashing young man passed by the counter. The clerks all seemed to know him, and several of the prettiest girls in the department smiled at him openly in a way that Faith thought very immodest. As he caught sight of the new packer he stopped abruptly and stared at her.

"Who the deuce is that?" Faith heard him say to one of the saleswomen, a girl whose cheeks were flaming with paint and whose appearance was that of a very vulgar person.

"I'm sure I don't know, Mr. Denton," replied the girl, with a simper. "She's a new packer that was taken on this morning. I haven't heard her name, and I don't know as I want to."

"Oh, you're jealous of her, are you, Mag?" said the young man with a laugh. "Well, I don't wonder, for she is a peach. I'm in love with her this minute!"

"You're a flirt, all right, Mr. Denton," said the girl, with a pout. "I think she's as awkward as anything, and her color is abominable."

"She's as fresh as a daisy," was the young man's answer. "Forbes had an eye for beauty when he hired that lovely creature."

"You men have queer taste," snapped the saleswoman, angrily, but the young man had passed on, staring at Faith all the way. Miss Fairbanks greeted him with a bow that was positively servile.

"That's old Denton's son Jim," explained Miss Jennings to Faith as she handed up a check. "He's a regular masher. Comes in here every few days, just to flirt with the girls. They say he's very wild and costs his father a lot of money."

"He is very bold," was Faith's whispered answer. "Why, he stared at me as if I were a dummy instead of a lady."

"Oh, we are none of us ladies: we are only clerks," replied Miss Jennings, bitterly. "If we were to snub Jim Denton he would make a lot of trouble for us."

"Mercy!" cried Faith. "It doesn't seem possible! Why, there seems to be pitfalls on every side for the girl who earns her own living."

Miss Fairbanks was coming, so the conversation was ended abruptly.

Miss Jennings went back to a customer who had just stopped at the counter.

"Show me some yellow ribbon, right away, miss," she said, very sharply. "I want to match this sample. Here, take a good look at it!"

Faith glanced down and saw that the customer was an ignorant-looking woman. She had on tawdry clothing and a lot of cheap jewelry.

Miss Jennings took the sample and glanced at it sharply.

"Do you wish exactly the same shade and width?" she asked, very politely.

"Of course! What did you suppose I brought the sample for if I don't?" cried the woman. "You must be a dunce to ask such a question!"

Faith felt her cheeks grow hot at this arrogant insult, but Miss Jennings replied as quietly as ever, "I cannot give you the same shade nor the same width exactly, madam. This is the nearest I have."

She handed her a roll that was a little different from the sample.

"But you must have it! Look again!" commanded the woman, angrily. "You are just trying to save yourself trouble, you lazy hussy!"

Miss Jennings turned very indifferently and called to another of the saleswomen:

"Miss Jones, have we any number twelve lemon in reserve? Here's a sample, and this lady is anxious to match it."

Miss Jones glanced at the sample that Miss Jennings was holding.

"You know very well that we are all out of that," she replied, sharply. "How often have I told you not to bother me with such questions!"

Miss Jennings handed the sample to the customer without the slightest trace of emotion.

"The 'head of stock' says we have none. I trust you will believe her, madam."

The woman snatched her sample and hurried away, while Miss Jennings went to another customer as calmly as though nothing had happened.

Faith drew a long breath. Her cheeks were fairly tingling. She glanced about a little to see whether any one else had noticed the transaction.

The clerks were all moving about in their automatic way. It was plain that such occurrences as this amounted to nothing.

Suddenly Faith's glance rested on a young man who was standing in the aisle where he could watch her every movement.

As their eyes met he raised his hat and smiled at her brazenly.

Faith gasped for breath. Her insulter was young Denton.

CHAPTER VI
FAITH DISCOVERS A FRESH HORROR

Faith dropped her eyes to her desk so that she would not see the fellow, but she could still feel the insulting gaze that was bent upon her.

She was glad when a great crowd of shoppers came surging in at the big doors, for the afternoons were always far busier than the mornings at this establishment.

Faith soon began to wonder if the goods could possibly come up to be wrapped very much faster. Her arms as well as her back were aching. The clerks were screaming for cash girls every other minute, for besides the packer above each counter there were a number of others at different points throughout the store and all were as busy as bees through the rush hours.

"There's no rest for the weary."

It was Miss Jennings who spoke. She was talking to a customer, a fine-looking old lady.

"I expect there isn't, dear," said the lady, pleasantly. "And you do look fagged out—I declare if you don't. I hope you get good pay for standing all day behind this counter!"

Miss Jennings laughed in her harsh, dry way.

"I won't shock you by telling you what I get," she said wearily. "But if all my customers were like you it would not matter so much. It's a pleasure to wait upon you! I hope you'll come often."

"Dear, dear! Well, I'm sorry if they are not all kind to you," said the lady. "It is hard to have to work, but there is some good reason for it. It will all come right by and by; but tell me, child, what in the world is the matter?"

There was a terrible racket on the floor overhead. As the lady asked the question a perfect bedlam broke loose.

The next second the cry of "Fire!" was heard all over the building.

"Quick! Come behind the counter, madam!" cried Miss Jennings, trying to draw the old lady through the gate. "There's a panic on the stairs! The mob will sweep through here directly!"

In less than a minute her words came true. There was a fearful rush of feet overhead, then with shrill shrieks of fright great crowds of women and children swept down the stairway. These were swelled by a small army of male and female clerks, until the whole lower floor was filled with a mob of struggling, pushing, human beings.

Miss Jennings succeeded in dragging the kind old lady behind the counter, then she began pulling away her goods as quickly as possible.

"Quick, girls! Get out while you can!" cried a frightened voice. "The second floor is all on fire! The ceiling will fall in a minute!"

Faith glanced around to see who had spoken. She was surprised to see that it was Miss Fairbanks, the buyer. In the hour of danger this coarse woman had actually thought to warn her charges, but she vanished in a second without waiting to see who followed.

"It will be folly to attempt to get out now," Faith cried distinctly. "We would only be trampled to death! Wait a minute,—do, until the aisles get clearer!"

"Remain at your posts and look after your goods!" cried a voice that every one recognized as that of Mr. Gibson, the manager, "The fire amounts to nothing. It was a false alarm! Don't one of you dare to leave your counters!"

"Do you expect us to stay here and burn up?" cried a woman's voice. "Well, I, for one, won't do it! Come on, Miss Jennings!"

"Not a step!" answered Miss Jennings in her shrill, weak voice. "You are a fool to trust your life in that howling mob, Kate! Wait a minute; we'll get out all right if we keep our wits about us."

"That's right," called Faith, standing erect at her desk. "Keep cool, girls; we are perfectly safe as long as we keep behind the counters."

"You are a nervy one, miss," said a voice at her ear.

Faith turned and saw that young Denton was standing close behind her.

"It is the only thing to do," she said with perfect composure. "Those people are all crazy. See how they trample on each other!"

She was gazing over the store in a perfectly natural way. There was not a trace of fear or excitement upon her features.

"The floor managers are getting them under control, I think," said the young man, who, like Faith, was as cool and composed as possible. "There they go—the very last of them—and the floor is deserted. Ten to one there's no fire at all. I'll go up and investigate."

He sprang off the counter and bounded up the stairs. Faith could not help noticing that he was really a very manly fellow. She began to think that she had been mistaken regarding his insulting actions.

"There is no fire, I tell you!" called Mr. Gibson again. "It was only a puff of smoke on the second floor! Will people never learn to keep their heads at such times, I wonder!"

The most of the clerks were still behind the counters, and as the manager made this remark one of the oldest men in the store raised his head and answered him.

"Our customers probably know our facilities for fighting a fire," he said sneeringly. "The place is a regular death-trap. No wonder they ran from it!"

"Keep your news to yourself, Block, if you please!" said Mr. Gibson quickly.

Some one called him at that instant or his reprimand would probably have been sharper.

Faith had heard both remarks, and so had the old lady, who was still standing beside Miss Jennings behind the ribbon counter.

"Is that true? Is the store such a fire-trap?" asked the old lady quickly. "Dear, dear, what a place to cage a lot of human beings!"

"The fire department has ordered the boss to put in more apparatus a dozen times that I know of," answered Miss Jennings, promptly, "but the building is insured and so is the stock. What do they care about us! We must take our chances!"

"Well, I guess the danger is over now, so I'll go," said the lady. "Thank you, my dear, for your kindness. I wish I could do something to help you."

"You have helped me with your sympathy," said Miss Jennings, quickly.

"You shall see me again," was the old lady's reply. "As a Christian woman, I must look into this matter."

She went away after shaking hands with Miss Jennings and smiling up at Faith in a friendly manner.

The clerks who had rushed down from the second floor at the alarm of fire were coming back slowly with a shamed look on their faces.

They trooped back up the stairs to their different departments just as a big sign was posted before the main entrance, stating that there was no fire in the building.

It was an exciting half hour, but through it all Faith stood erect, ready and calmly waiting for anything that might happen. In the very midst of the commotion her quick eyes detected a fresh horror. She saw a clerk at a neighboring counter grab a handsome piece of jewelry and secrete it in her pocket with the rapidity of lightning.

When order was at last restored Faith was in a most distressed frame of mind. She was dreading through sheer pity what she knew to be her duty.

"All over, Faith, and no lives lost," called Miss Jennings softly.

She was as absolutely colorless and apathetic as ever.

"Oh, Mary," whispered Faith, "there's something I must tell you."

She bent down from her desk after looking about sharply for the buyer.

"Don't mind about Fairbanks, she has bolted!" said Miss Jennings with a laugh. "You can trust the heads of departments to save their own bacon!"

"But, she thought of us, too; you heard her, Mary," said Faith. "Poor thing, she may be irritable, but she isn't bad-hearted."

"I ain't so sure about that—but what is it, Faith? There will be no customers for some time, probably, so you have a right to talk to me."

Faith leaned a little lower so she could whisper in her ear.

"I just saw one of the clerks steal something," she said, "It was during the excitement. She has it in her pocket."

"Oh, that's nothing!"

Miss Jennings spoke as indifferently as ever.

"Why, what do you mean?" Faith gasped in astonishment. "You surely do not mean that you approve of stealing!"

"Approve of it, no!" answered Miss Jennings slowly. "But it doesn't concern you or me, either, Faith. The girl was probably desperate. I do not blame her!"

"Oh, Mary!"

Faith's words were redolent of bitter anguish. For the first time since they met she drew a little away from her.

"You don't understand, Faith," said the other quickly. She had noticed the movement, and her tone showed that she was pained by it.

"I'm afraid I don't."

Faith said the words coldly. "I certainly don't understand dishonesty in the very least. I may be wrong, but I cannot excuse it. It is my duty to report that girl, and I shall certainly do it."

"You shall not!"

Miss Jennings had lost her apathy and indifference for once. She was locking Faith steadily in the eye, her own fairly burning with anger.

"See here, Faith," she went on, "you have a whole lot to learn, and I guess I am just as well qualified to teach you as any one. What you don't know about dishonesty would fill a whole library of books. Promise me that you will say nothing about that matter until to-morrow, at least. Promise, Faith. It will do no harm. If you are a Christian you must have charity."

Faith gazed at her earnestly for the space of a second. There was something besides anger in her new friend's eagerness.

CHAPTER VII
FRESH GLIMPSES OF EVIL

"I promise," said Faith, after another moment's hesitation. "I will hear what you have to say on the subject, Mary, but I am sure I shall still think it right to report that theft to-morrow."

Miss Jennings turned away with a relieved expression. The woman she had called "Kate" was just coming back behind the counter.

"I've lost my job through my stupidity," she said sullenly. "Gibson says I am discharged for being impudent to him."

"I'm sorry, but you might have known," replied Miss Jennings shortly. "Still, you haven't lost much; perhaps you'll get something better."

"Well, I hope so, but there's not much chance at this season," said the woman. "Six dollars a week was better than nothing. It's more than I can make by taking in washing."

"Oh, you surely won't have to do that!" cried Faith involuntarily. She had been listening to their conversation without realizing it.

The woman glanced up at her and gave a sharp laugh.

"That, or worse," she said coarsely. "I can't starve to death, can I?"

There was no mistaking what she meant. Her words sent a thrill of horror through every fibre of Faith's body.

"She surely did not mean that," she whispered to Miss Jennings as soon as the saleswoman had gone.

"Why not?" asked Miss Jennings in her bitterest manner.

For the second time that day Faith drew back with swift motion, but this time her companion did not appear to notice it.

"She's got a sick husband and three children," she said sharply; "and it's no fault of hers that she can't earn an honest living. I tell you, Faith, that you have lots to learn. I'm sorry you must learn it all in a lump, of course, but the sooner it is learned the sooner you'll get used to it."

She breathed a deep sigh as she turned away. For a moment her real feeling showed above her indifference.

"Get used to it—never!" cried Faith, almost hysterically. "And you are not used to it, either, Mary; it is killing you this minute!"

"Perhaps you are right," said Miss Jennings, slowly, then as the customers were gradually drifting back into the store she went forward to wait upon them with her usual indifference.

For the next half hour Faith was very busy. The excitement had passed, leaving no trace behind it.

At exactly six o'clock a big gong was sounded. Faith was so tired and nervous that she almost cried for joy when she heard it.

"It has been the hardest day of my life," she said to Miss Jennings as they reached the cloak-room.

"Well, you'll have many such if you stay here long," was the reply. "There are nothing but hard days for the slaves of Denton, Day & Co."

There was a crowd of women and girls waiting at the lavatory basins, and as Faith caught sight of the towels she turned away with a shudder.

"You'll have to go home with dirty hands, Faith, but you musn't mind that; we wouldn't get out of here until midnight if we waited our turn at those basins."

Miss Jennings was putting on her hat as she spoke, and as Faith started to look for hers the clerk whom young Denton had called "Mag" came slowly up to them.

"Heard the news, eighty-nine?"

She asked Miss Jennings the question, but she was looking straight at Faith. There was a gleam in her eye that was very unpleasant.

"What news, Maggie?" asked Miss Jennings, noticing the look at once. She knew the girl's disposition, and almost dreaded what was coming.

"Old Forbes was robbed of five hundred dollars! Some one stole it from his desk early yesterday morning. There's pretty good proof already as to who was the thief. I wouldn't stand in her shoes for double the money!"

She was still watching Faith with her eyes half closed. Miss Jennings was too shrewd to be deceived a minute as to her actual meaning.

"Well, you'll save yourself trouble by keeping your mouth shut," she said, crossly, "it dont pay to meddle with such matters as that, Maggie, especially if you happen to be living under a cloud yourself. Somebody might take a notion to turn the tables on you, you know. I'd as as soon be a thief as some other things I might mention."

There was a sneer in her tones that was unmistakable. Faith turned just in time to catch its full meaning.

"Oh, you needn't preach!" cried the other angrily. "Any one can see you're fairly green with envy, eighty-nine! You'd give a whole lot to be able to flirt with the boys, but, as Jim Denton says, you are too pale and skinny!"

"For shame!"

It was Faith who spoke the words. She was facing the brazen-faced girl with her eyes blazing angrily.

"How dare you speak like that to a poor, sick girl? Have you no heart in your bosom, no decency or conscience! It does not seem possible to me that girls can be so hateful toward each other. Are we not all sisters, who have been commanded to love one another?"

There was silence for just a second as Faith finished speaking, then a loud, coarse laugh broke from Maggie Brady's lips.

"Oh, Lord! Hear her, girls! Hear the little preacher in petticoats! Isn't she eloquent, the pretty thing! Why, she ought to be a corporal in the Salvation Army!"

There was a roar of laughter at the rude girl's words, during which Miss Jennings caught Faith by the arm and half dragged her from the cloak-room.

"Come, Faith, let us go! This is no place for you. That girl is the most brazen hussy in the whole establishment, and that's saying a good deal, as you'll find out later!"

They hurried out into the street as quickly as possible. Faith was almost crying with indignation when they reached the sidewalk.

"Now, brace up, dear; it's all over for to-day," said Miss Jennings. "You'll soon get used to it; that's exactly what every one of us have had to go through with, but the girls are not all like Mag; there are lots of nice ones. She wasn't so bad, either, until Jim Denton noticed her."

"Is he her sweetheart?" asked Faith as soon as she could control her voice. "I heard them talking together and I am sure she loves him."

Miss Jennings gave vent to one of her harshest laughs.

"Jim Denton is a wicked young man," she said very slowly. "He cares no more for Maggie than he does for lots of the others, but she's such a fool she can't see it, and that shows, of course, that she's pretty badly gone on him."

"You mean that she loves him?" questioned Faith, who was not very familiar with shop-girl slang.

"Well, you can't call it love, exactly," explained Miss Jennings, "but it's the best she's got. She thinks she loves him."

The girls had walked a couple of blocks and were waiting for a car. They were glad to find that they lived near each other. The same street car would land them a short distance from their homes, which were modest flats in the cheapest portion of Harlem.

As they hailed the car, Faith's quick eye caught a glimpse of a man who seemed to be following them.

As he sprang on the rear platform of the car she called her companion's attention to him.

"It's Bob Hardy, one of our detectives," said Miss Jennings, wonderingly. "Why, he lives in Jersey. He must be following somebody."

Faith looked at her a moment before she spoke again.

"I wonder if there is any truth in what that girl said about the robbery in the office. I've been thinking of it ever since. She looked at me so funny! And see, Mary, that detective is watching me, too, he has hardly taken his eyes off me since we entered the car. It can't be possible that they think I took the money, can it? You know I was in the office early yesterday morning."

She spoke so timidly that Miss Jennings gave her a sharp glance. Then she turned involuntarily and looked at the detective.

"God help you if Hardy is after you," she whispered with a shudder. "That fellow is a fiend about making arrests. He'd accuse his own mother of stealing, I believe, if he thought he could win the regard of old Forbes by doing it!"

CHAPTER VIII
A FIENDISH PROPOSITION

When Faith left the car Bob Hardy followed her. He made no attempt to conceal the fact that he was watching her, and when Faith had reached the middle of a block of vacant lots he quickened his steps and was soon beside her.

"Just a minute, miss," he said, tapping her lightly on the shoulder.

Faith wheeled around and confronted him with cold dignity.

"Well, what do you wish with me, sir?" she asked quietly. "I noticed that you were following me. Have you had orders to do so?"

"Not exactly, miss," said the detective, a little disconcertedly, "but you are in a pretty bad fix over that money affair, and I just thought I'd put you on your guard as a sort of favor."

"What?"

Faith's voice fairly vibrated with indignation. "Explain yourself, sir. I do not understand you?"

"Oh, if you insist," said the detective with a disagreeable leer, "I won't be so unkind as to disappoint a lady."

He stepped a little to one side as he spoke, and his eyes wandered scrutinizingly over Faith's lovely face and figure.

"You see," he continued, "you are badly tangled up in that affair at the office; in fact, to be plain, Mr. Forbes thinks that you stole the five hundred dollars, and it will go hard with you when he gets back to biz; that's why I wanted to warn you."

"Indeed!"

Faith's head towered above the detective's as she spoke.

"You are very kind, Mr. Detective; but, as I have stolen no money, nor anything else, I have no fear of Mr. Forbes, or any need of your most extraordinary warning. You will please allow me to pass and not follow me any farther. It is no sign because I am working in a store that I am not a lady and entitled to courtesy."

She started to pass him, but with a stride the fellow was before her.

"Not so fast, my fine lady," he cried with a sneer. "You don't know me, I guess. I don't let thieves escape me so easily."

"How dare you?" cried Faith, her face flaming with anger.

"Oh, I dare anything," retorted the detective, "especially where my reputation is at stake! I've got orders from Forbes to catch that thief, and, as you are the easiest bird to catch, I'm just going to bag you—that's all there is about it. I'll swear that I found this wad of bills in your pocket, see!"

He drew a roll of money from his pocket and flourished it before her as he spoke.

"Oh, you would never be so wicked, so dastardly, as that!" cried Faith. "Have you no sense of honor, no manliness about you?"

Her words were so appealing that the detective winced a little. His keen eyes shifted uneasily. He could not face her.

"I offered to warn you," he muttered at last. "There's a way out of the fix if you are a mind to take it."

"But I am in no fix!" protested Faith. "I have done no wrong! How dare you accuse me!"

The detective went on as though she had not spoken.

"There's a way out of it, miss; you have only to say the word. I know a gent that's in love with you this very minute. He'll fix things with old Forbes—he's got lots of dough. Just you promise to be agreeable and I'll hush the whole thing up to-morrow."

As he made this fiendish suggestion he eyed the girl sharply.

Each change in her expression seemed to render her more beautiful. For a moment she was dazed and almost powerless to speak, then, as a great wave of color swept up to her very brow, she fairly hissed her answer in a scorching whisper.

"You coward! You cur! Go at once and leave me! Make what accusations you like—I am afraid of you no longer! In God will I place my trust, and He will not forsake me! Go, I say, and think well over what you are doing. Remember that there is One above you who is watching your evil deeds and as surely as He will punish the wicked so will He protect the innocent!"

As she spoke the last words she walked hastily away.

Bob Hardy stared after her stupidly, but did not attempt to follow her.

"Well, what did she say?" asked a voice at his elbow.

A well-dressed man of middle age had walked slowly across the street and stood waiting impatiently for Hardy's answer.

The detective drew a long breath and shrugged his shoulders a little.

"Oh, she's a high flyer," he answered, cautiously. "It will take time to clip her wings and tame her, captain, but don't you worry a bit. I'll earn your fifty dollars."

"As you have earned several other fifties," said the "captain," smiling. "Oh, well, you are in the right place for just such work. It's dead easy for you, Hardy. Why, those girls would all of them jump at the chance of getting out from behind those counters, but the deuce of it is that it's only the new ones who are pretty."

"Well, you've picked out the prettiest now, all right," laughed Hardy. "But I expect I shall have to scare her a little. She's not only proud as Lucifer, but she's chock full of religion. Says God will protect her and all that sort of thing."

The well-dressed "captain" threw back his head and roared.

"God will trouble Himself a lot about her, I'm thinking," he said, chuckling. "He is so given to looking after those half-starved creatures! Why, the Devil is the shop girls' best friend, if they only knew it."

"He stands by us pretty well, too, eh! captain?" said Hardy. "But I must be getting home, as I live way over in Jersey. I'll report to-morrow night at your place downtown. She'll be less religious by that time if she sees that God has gone back on her, I guess."

"You mean that you will press the charge against her and have them send her to jail? That's going pretty far, Hardy; but I'll leave it to your judgment."

"Oh, pshaw! She'll be tractable before it comes to that pass, captain. I've seen girls before. I know how to handle 'em."

The two men parted, Hardy going to his home in Jersey, while the man whom he had called "captain" went in the direction of Fifth avenue.

When he arrived at his magnificent bachelor apartments he let himself in with a latch-key. His colored valet was busy in one of the rooms packing his master's clothing into two traveling bags.

"Well, Dave," said the captain, gayly, "we will have a fine trip South, I fancy; but don't hurry with that packing. Let it go for a day. I've decided not to start as soon as I intended."

"All right, sah; I'll drop it right quick, sah," said the negro. "Yere's a letter, sah, dat was brung 'bout an hour ago. I dun tole de boy dat you would anser it at your leesyur, sah."

Captain Paul Deering laughed at his servant's language. Dave always used big words and the most extravagant manners when he came in contact with other people's servants.

"By Jove!" exclaimed the captain, as he opened the letter. "It's from my lawyer, Dave, telling me that my sister has been found. She is living here in the city, and is a widow with one daughter."

"Yo' doan' say so, sah!"

Dave was standing with his mouth wide open to indicate his interest in the news. He had been with the captain so long that he was very deep in his confidences.

"Yes, she's here in town, and has been for years, and to think I've been here, too, and didn't know it! You see, Dave, I ran away from home when she was only a young girl. When the home was broken up I lost track of her completely. Now there's a snug little fortune waiting for her that she should have had five years ago, but perhaps it's just as well it's been accumulating interest all the time."

"An' yourn has bin a losin' interes'," replied the negro, grinning. "I neber see money slip troo' a man's fingers so fas' as it do troo' yourn, capting, dat's a fac'."

"Oh, I get the worth of it as I go along, Dave," laughed the captain, "but I suppose I've got to go out again now and call on my new-found sister."

He glanced at the address which the lawyer had given him.

"Pshaw! That's too bad," he said, impatiently. "If I had only known this two hours sooner! Why, I've just come from that very locality, and it's way up in Harlem."

As he reached for his hat there was a sharp ring at his door-bell.

"Dat's Dr. Graham, sah; I knows dat ring ob his," said the valet quickly. "Dat mean, sah, you doan' call on no sister dis ebenin'."

CHAPTER IX
THE PLEA OF MISS JENNINGS

When Faith Marvin entered her mother's four-room flat on the top floor of a dingy brick building she was almost out of breath from indignation and rapid walking.

She tried to calm herself a little before her mother saw her, for Mrs. Marvin was on the verge of nervous prostration.

When Faith looked into the little parlor she saw what she dreaded most, her mother lying on the sofa suffering from a terrible headache.

"I must say absolutely nothing," whispered Faith to herself; "but what if that fellow should follow me home! Oh, it would be terrible! Terrible! I am sure it would kill her!"

She washed her face and hands and smoothed her hair, then went quietly into the parlor and kissed her mother.

"Oh, Faith," cried the sick woman, sharply.

"How did you get along, dear? Were they kind to you in that dreadful store, or will they kill my daughter, as they did my husband?"

"Hush, mother; don't say anything like that, there's a dear," said Faith quickly. "Don't let your mind dwell so steadily on unpleasant things, and just as soon as your head is better I'll tell you all about it."

"Tell me now, Faith, I insist," cried her mother, irritably. "I must know the truth at once. Just think, dear, I have lain here all day worrying about you, my child! It has been the hardest day of your life! I feel it and I can see it."

She was gazing at Faith with a keen, penetrating glance. It would have been cruel to have kept her in ignorance any longer.

"Well, then, lie down, dear, and I'll begin at the beginning," said Faith gently, "and you must promise not to ask questions until I have finished."

She laid her mother back on the sofa and began her tale, but she took care to touch upon some things very lightly and leave others out of her narration altogether.

When she had finished her mother still lay silent for a few minutes, then she suddenly sat up straight and stared at her daughter.

"It is a thousand times worse than I thought," she said slowly. "Although your father told me a great deal about the evils that exist in business places. Why, those men are criminals and nothing less! They are destroying women's souls as well as starving their bodies, and all to swell their own bank accounts and ride in carriages. Oh, it is shameful! And to think that nothing can be done to stop it."

"But something must be done! Something shall be done!" cried Faith stoutly. "There is one power alone that can conquer all evil. We must invoke that power upon this dreadful curse, and God has promised that the prayer of faith shall not go unanswered."

"Oh, child, can you not see how foolish all that is?" asked her mother irritably. "As if prayer was needed for what God can see for Himself! If He wished things different He could easily change them. I have no faith in His goodness, His love or His mercy."

The tears sprang to Faith's eyes, but the words did not surprise her. She laid them to the weakness of her mother's physical condition.

"Some day you will see it differently, dear little mother," she said, sweetly. "You are still resentful for the injury which you have suffered. When that spirit has been conquered your faith will return. 'All things work together for good to them that love Him.'"

"Do you mean that your dear father's death was intended for my good?" her mother almost screamed. "Do you see mercy, child, in such cruel injustice, injustice that allows the rich to prosper in their evil ways and puts the knife of poverty to the throat of the deserving? No! a thousand times no! I will not believe it! Your father was an honest man doing a legitimate business. Those sharks opened their store and put in a book department. They undercut his figures even when it was a loss to do so, knowing that in the end they would ruin him and drive him out of their path forever! What followed? You know only too well, my poor, fatherless daughter. In a fit of despondency he killed himself; the man who had done no wrong—except to lose his courage, and they, Denton, Day & Co., have accumulated millions. They have his blood on their hands as they have the blood of many others!"

The poor woman was rocking herself back and forth as she talked, while Faith could only bury her head in the sofa pillows and pray silently for wisdom.

She knew that the frenzy would wear away soon. Her mother's strength could not stand the strain of such agony many minutes.

"I can understand that girl stealing the jewelry, Faith," she went on more calmly, "It was a terrible thing to do, but she doubtless justified herself in doing it. And the woman who is going from bad is worse—oh, she has my sympathy, poor wretch! She is hopeless, discouraged; she does not know what she is doing."

Faith got up silently and went out into the kitchen. In a few moments she came back with a cup of tea for her mother.

In a second her action had reaped its results. The mother instinct asserted itself. Mrs Marvin suddenly remembered that Faith had had no supper.

"I am to have a visitor soon, mother," said Faith with a smile, while her mother was getting the supper, "Miss Jennings is coming in later. She lives only two blocks from the corner."

"She is a consumptive, I think you said. I shall be glad to see her," said Mrs. Marvin, "and I'll try, Faith, to calm my nerves, and not force my bitterness on another."

Faith smiled very sadly at her mother's words.

"Miss Jennings is far more bitter than you can ever be, mother dear," she said slowly. "She is almost callous, while you are still smarting with anguish."

For the next half-hour Faith busied herself with their frugal supper. Before the meal was over she was pleased to see that her mother was becoming more composed and natural. When Miss Jennings came in both ladies greeted her warmly. There was a hectic glow in her cheeks, and she coughed almost constantly.

Mrs. Marvin left the two girls together at an early hour. She had kept her promise and been remarkably cheerful.

"Now, Faith, to business," said Miss Jennings, as soon as they were alone. "I want to tell you why you must not report that clerk's theft to-morrow."

Faith drew her chair a little nearer and prepared to listen. She was beginning to understand her friend's character a little better.

"In the first place," began Miss Jennings, "we will consider the girl. I know her well. You need not describe her. What I know about her is this: She is the daughter of a criminal. Her father was a pickpocket, he died in prison. Now I ask you, Faith, what can you expect from this girl? According to your Bible are not 'the iniquities' of the fathers visited upon the children, and are the innocents to blame for their undesirable inheritance? Furthermore, that girl's mother was what we call an outcast. Can you reasonably look for morality of any sort in the offspring of such an infamous union? You do not answer, because you cannot! I defy any of your Christians to straighten out this matter. The viciousness of most children is their only endowment, unless we add the poverty, the diseases and the hopelessness that go with it. Now to consider her environments and her temptations in that store. She is working for thieves, why should she not steal? She is working for successful people, why should she not take example of their methods. These things seem harsh and hard to you, Faith, but they are actual facts, just as you will surely see them. If you report that girl what will be the result? Listen, here it is, the outcome in a nutshell. You will be reporting to robbers that they are being robbed, not of their lives, their liberties and their honors, as they rob us, but of a paltry piece of jewelry, which they have bought out of their enormous profits. You will, no doubt, lose for the girl a position which has the semblance of respectability, and like poor Kate Travers, she will go from bad to worse, only, unlike Kate, she will have no pure motive. Then, lastly, to consider your own position in the matter, from that standpoint which you choose to call your Christian duty—"

She stopped to cough, and Faith broke in upon her.

"I know what you would say. You think by reporting her crime I will only be driving her to more vicious depths, whereas, by protecting her from the punishment she deserves I may be able to influence her toward a better life. Oh, Mary, I thank you! You have shown me my error. Say no more to me to-night about censuring any one for their wrongdoing! It grows more wonderful every moment that the girls are as good as they are. God help them, they are innocent! It is all the fault of conditions! If we could only strike at the root of it all, Mary."

"We would have to go back many years and generations, I'm afraid," whispered Miss Jennings. "But at present we need go no further than the heads of that firm—for Denton, Day & Forbes are the roots in this case, from which emanate the evils which are destroying us soul and body."

CHAPTER X
A STARTLING SUGGESTION

The gossip in the cloak-room was at its height the next morning when Faith entered promptly at half-past seven. She looked around for Miss Jennings, but did not see her. The next moment her attention was attracted by a short conversation between two of the saleswomen.

"Well, Jack Forbes is dead at last, poor fellow," said one of them, "and they say that his father is all broke up over it. Jack was his ideal always. It's sure to go hard with him."

"He deserves his trouble if ever any one did," was the indifferent answer. "He's made life miserable for lots of young men who were just as worthy as Jack ever was and just as much beloved by their mothers and fathers."

"Well, he's being punished now all right. They say he looks like a ghost. Wonder if he'll have the good taste to close the store! Or will he keep open that day to make funeral expenses?"

There was a shout of laughter after this remark, and Faith was surprised to see how many of the girls joined in it.

"Oh, here you are," said a voice at her side.

She turned and was delighted to see Miss Jennings.

"How pale you look, Mary! Did you tire yourself too much last night?" she asked quickly. "Really dear, you should have stayed at home. You are sick abed this very minute!"

"That would mean a dollar, my dear Faith," said Miss Jennings sharply. "I've lost three already this month so far and as I'm liable to need a coffin soon I must keep at work and earn it!"

"Don't, Mary!" cried Faith, in genuine distress. "Don't joke about such things, dear. I can't bear to hear you."

"As well laugh as cry," said Miss Jennings shortly; "but I hear that Jack Forbes is dead. I'm in hopes the firm will show proper decency by giving us a holiday."

"Oh, they'll do that all right, if it is only for the looks of the thing," cried one of the girls who had overheard her. "You can trust them to keep up appearances before the public, even if they dock us a day's pay in order to square it."

"They would never do that!" cried Faith in dismay.

"They'd do it if they dared," was the answer; "they are not above it."

"There is Mr. Gibson now," whispered another girl as the form of the manager appeared in the doorway.

"The store will be closed to-morrow," he said, shortly, "so you girls want to be smart and make all the sales you can to-day. Remember that you are expected to do your best in such emergencies."

As he went away the clerks all looked at each other.

"That sounded just like Forbes himself," giggled one of the girls. "I'll bet ten dollars he sent down that message."

"Well, we all get a day off anyway," said another, "and for my part I'm glad to laugh once while Old Forbes is crying. The shoe is on the other foot generally and we girls do the weeping."

"I wonder if that detective will annoy me to-day," whispered Faith to her friend. She had already told her of the proposition which Hardy had made to her.

"I wonder who the fellow is who has got his eye on you," said Miss Jennings, soberly. "It's the same old story. They think because we are poor that we are to be bought and sold like puppets. You'd be surprised, Faith, to know how men look upon us girls, but never mind about it, dear; Hardy can't do anything until the superintendent comes back, and by that time Mr. Watkins may have found the money."

"Who is Mr. Watkins?" asked Faith, who had quite forgotten the young man.

"He's the superintendent's lackey, but they call him an assistant," said Miss Jennings, with a slight blush. "He's a remarkably fine young man who would be honest if he could, but, poor soul, he's like the rest of us—tied hand and foot! If he expresses an honest opinion, out he goes into the street, and that means that not only himself but his mother would starve."

"I remember him now," said Faith; "he was in the superintendent's office when I applied for my position. I liked his looks; he seemed refined and honest. I wish I could help him, but—Oh, Mary, what's the matter?"

Miss Jennings had suddenly put her handkerchief to her lips. When she took it down there were blood stains upon it.

"Nothing, dear," she said as soon as she could speak, "only the last end of a hemorrhage that I had this morning."

"But do you have to work to-day? Is it really necessary?" urged Faith.

Miss Jennings turned to her quickly and opened her pocket-book. There were seventeen cents and a small photograph in the purse. Faith had just time to recognize the picture as that of Mr. Watkins when Miss Jennings closed the book with a flush of annoyance.

"That's all I've got to last out the week, Faith," she said between her coughs, "and I have a crippled brother at home, a last legacy from my parents."

She hurried up the stairs, with Faith close behind her. In five minutes the work of the day had begun; goods were being taken deftly from the shelves and displayed upon the counters.

Miss Fairbanks was on hand and as cross as ever. She went around like a virago and scolded nearly every one in her department.

When Maggie Brady came in she looked weary and jaded, and the paint on her face made her more conspicuous than ever.

During a lull in the business Faith heard her speaking to Miss Fairbanks in a tone that showed plainly that she was very confidential with the buyer.

"Jim Denton took me to the theatre last night and we had an elegant supper after. It cost him a pile, I tell you, for I just laid myself out to be expensive. It's the only way I have of getting square with the firm. What the old man makes his son blows in; that's right, ain't it, Fairbanks?" she winked at the woman as she finished.

"Sure," replied Miss Fairbanks in a lower tone; "but look out for him, Mag, there's a new star in the heavens. I wouldn't trust Jim Denton around the corner, and you wouldn't either if you were wiser."

"Oh, I'm not afraid of that, if that's what you mean," said the girl. She nodded her head in Faith's direction, but did not deign to look at her.

"She's a beauty all right," was the buyer's reply, "and she doesn't have to improve on nature a little bit, eh, Maggie?"

"She won't keep that color long in this store," sneered Miss Brady. "She'll fade like all the rest of us, and it won't take long either."

"Miss Fairbanks," gasped Miss Jennings from behind the counter, "I can't stand up any longer. You will have to excuse me."

"Well, you do look sick, so I suppose you can go. But as it is only ten o'clock I shall have to call it a full day, Miss Jennings."

"Call it anything you like," whispered Miss Jennings hoarsely; "only let me lie down, on the floor or anywhere."

Faith sprang down from her high perch without an instant of hesitation.

"Let me take her to the cloak-room, please, Miss Fairbanks," she begged. "Miss Jennings is my friend—do, please, let me take her."

"Nonsense! Get back to your desk this instant, packer! If she is too sick to go alone one of the cash girls can take her. Come, hurry along; there are customers coming."

Faith gave a despairing sob as she climbed back to her seat. Miss Jennings was desperately ill—she was sure of it.

Suddenly it occurred to her what a really brave fellow Mr. Watkins was. She had heard Mr. Forbes tell him to have Miss Jennings discharged, yet for two days he had disregarded the order.

That, and the picture of the young man in Miss Jennings' purse told Faith a story as plain as words could have done. The two were lovers, she was positive of it, she began to wonder if Mr. Watkins knew of his sweetheart's condition.

"Move faster there, packer!" called Miss Fairbanks crossly. "Can't you see the lady is waiting for her parcel while you are loitering?"

"Oh, I am in no hurry at all, madam," said a calm, lady-like voice. "Do not hurry the poor girl, please. She is probably tired."

"She has no right to be tired at this time in the morning"—Miss Fairbanks was trying to be polite, but her voice was still snappy.

"Are you never tired at this hour?" asked the lady, calmly. "I frequently wake tired, and from no especial reason. In this case I should think it surprising if she ever felt rested."

"Oh, they get used to it—we all do," said Miss Fairbanks, stammering. "Or, at least, we must do our work just the same. We are not supposed to have feelings."

"Pray, tell me who are your judges, madam?" The lady spoke more sharply. "Who dares to say that human beings who earn their living have no feelings?"

"Well, if they don't say so out loud that is what they think," replied the buyer. "Why, we'd be discharged before night if we were to complain of too much work. They want machines in these stores, and we are the nearest substitutes."

"Well, why don't you all rebel and force your employers to think differently? Mind, I don't tell you to do it. I am just asking for information."

"It would do no good; we would simply lose our places, and for each one of us there would be ten applicants to-morrow."

Miss Fairbanks spoke the truth, and she spoke it sadly.

For the second time Faith was inclined to think that the woman was not bad-hearted.

"The law should step in and regulate such matters," said the lady. "So much authority should not be allowed to a few human beings. A few arrests for manslaughter would not be amiss. I have just seen one woman who is being killed by this slavery, and there are plenty more behind these counters."

"But no jury could convict our employers, if that is what you mean." Miss Fairbanks was gasping over the startling suggestion.

"I'm not so sure," said the lady thoughtfully. "If they could see what I have just seen they might possibly do it There is a young woman dying this minute down in that villainous cloak-room."

With a smothered groan Faith sprang swiftly to the floor.

"It is Mary—my friend," she cried out in agony. "No, Miss Fairbanks, you shall not stop me! I will go to Miss Jennings!"

CHAPTER XI
A DEATH IN THE CLOAK-ROOM

When Faith reached the cloak-room she found a scene of the wildest confusion. A number of clerks and cash girls were surrounding Miss Jennings, who lay on the floor upon a pile of wraps which they had hurriedly thrown down for her. Mr. Gibson, the manager, was bending over her with a glass of water in his hand, and was giving orders right and left in an excited manner.

"Go for a doctor, some one!" he cried. "No, get an ambulance—that will be better! The officer on the corner will call one for you. It will never do to have her die here! The newspapers would all get it, and goodness only knows what they would say about us."

He raised his head as he spoke and found himself face to face with the new packer in the ribbon department. She was as white as chalk and her eyes were flaming with anger.

"How dare you send her to a hospital when she is so ill?" she whispered, sharply. "Get a physician here at once, sir, and a glass of wine instead of water."

She pushed her way through the group of frightened girls and looked upon her friend, whom she saw at once was unconscious from weakness.

"Stand back a little, girls, and give her air," she cried, firmly. "There is none too much ventilation in this place, Mr. Gibson; quick—lower the windows if you can, sir."

Without dreaming of disobeying, Mr. Gibson sprang to the window. There was something so commanding in her manner that she fairly over-awed him. The next moment he had dispatched cash girls for a doctor and some wine, even taking the money out of his own pocket to pay for the cordial.

Faith had succeeded in clearing a circle about the fainting girl, and was just looking for something with which to fan her, when two people—a man and a woman—entered the door of the cloak-room, and stopped short when they saw the unusual spectacle.

"It is just as I thought—she is dying," said the woman, softly.

Faith recognized the voice at once. It was the lady whom she had just left talking to Miss Fairbanks at the ribbon counter.

"You see, Mr. Denton, my words have come true! You are killing these young women by overwork and bad air, yet you dare to resent any interference in the matter."

Faith was kneeling by Miss Jennings now and had raised her head to her lap. There was a quiver of the girl's eyelids. When the wine came at last she was able to swallow it.

"This is dreadful!" said Mr. Denton, in a tone of genuine distress. "Here, Mr. Gibson, do all you possibly can for that young woman, and for Heaven's sake, try to keep this out of the newspapers."

"Can I help you, dear?" said the lady, going over to where Faith sat by her friend, "or am I merely exhausting the air that the poor child should be breathing? You were a brave girl to come to her rescue as you did. If any trouble results from it, be sure and let me know it."

She dropped her card into Faith's lap, and left the place with Mr. Denton.

The doctor was just entering and there was no spare room. She had seen at a glance that Faith could do all that was needed.

A few minutes later Miss Jennings opened her eyes. When she saw Faith bending over her she smiled very happily.

"You are better, dear, aren't you?" whispered Faith, as she tried to return the smile.

Miss Jennings shook her head gently. "I am satisfied," was her low answer.

"But I want you to be happy, Mary," cried Faith, who saw death in the poor girl's face. "Look up, dear; there is One who loves you. Can you not believe it?"

"I trust it is so," said the dying girl, faintly, "I have not believed, but I may have been mistaken."

"You were indeed, Mary, but you were not to blame! Poor child, yours has been a sad lot, but there is happiness coming."

There were stifled sobs from many of the girls who were standing in frightened groups about the room. The hush upon each lip spoke only too plainly of death's presence.

"Poor Dick!" sighed Miss Jennings. "If it were not for Dick—"

Dick was the crippled brother who was her only charge.

"I will take him to live with me, Mary," whispered Faith, nobly. "My mother will love him and so will I—but what is it, dear?"

Miss Jennings was trying to say something more. Her voice was so low that only Faith could hear it.

"Will He forgive indifference, rebellion, distrust?"

"Though your sins are as scarlet, He shall wash them white, dear Mary. As we forgive our enemies, so He will forgive us."

The dying girl raised her eyes. Strangely enough their gaze rested upon the face of Mr. Denton.

He had come back to the scene only a moment before, and for perhaps the first time in his life, pangs of remorse were seizing him.

"I—forgive—" murmured the poor girl, still gazing at Mr. Denton. Her eyes closed slowly as she spoke.

With a fearful groan, Mr. Denton fled from the place.

The physician had done what he could, but his efforts were useless. Another life had gone out at the very dawning of its day; crushed out by the injustice and the greed of fellow-beings. Faith choked back her sobs as well as she could, and looked on in amazement at what followed the tragedy. An undertaker was called and placed in charge of the body, and the utmost concern seemed to be felt about all the arrangements, especially by Mr. Gibson, who had been put in charge of the matter by the firm.

Faith would not have understood such a sudden "change of heart" if she had not been enlightened by one of the other women.

"They know it's bound to get into the papers," she whispered, "so they are making a big bluff, you know. They don't really care about Miss Jennings."

Faith put on her hat without waiting to hear more; Such hypocrisy as this completely overcame her.

Miss Fairbanks was not consulted regarding her movements now, for the young girl quite forgot the rules and regulations of the establishment. As quick as she could she started to go up-town in search of the humble rooms where she knew she would find the crippled boy whom she had taken under her protection.

As she left the store a young man joined her. She gave a sharp glance at his face. It was Mr. Watkins.

Involuntarily the young girl extended her hand, and in that sympathetic clasp both knew that their love for the dead girl was mutual, and that forever after between them would be the firmest friendship.

Mr. Watkins insisted upon accompanying Faith on her errand of mercy, and as he seemed to need her tender consolation and sympathy, Faith was glad to allow him to share her mission.

He had heard of his sweetheart's death only through the gossip of the store, so Faith told him of Mary's calm resignation, and her belief that she died happy in the faith of a true Christian.

The crippled boy, Dick, was a sweet little fellow of six years, and in spite of the added expense, Mrs. Marvin was glad to have him with her. He would give her something to think of, she said, in the long days to come, when Faith would be away at business. She set about to comfort the little fellow at once.

Faith was too disturbed to go back to the store that day, and as it was to be closed the next day on account of the funeral of young Mr. Forbes, she had time to think over the outlook for the future.

"I am sure Mr. Denton is not a bad man, mother," she said, as they sat with Mr. Watkins in the little parlor. "His face showed the deepest agony. I am sure he has a heart. Oh, if only I could reach it, perhaps things would be different."

"But you say that lady, the Government Inspector, was with him at the time. His distress may have been feigned," answered her mother, suspiciously.

"I don't think so, mother, for there were tears in his eyes. I think he is merely neglectful. He leaves the consideration for employees entirely to his partners."

"Many business men are that way," remarked her mother, after a minute. "They are so concerned about their financial matters that they ignore what is more sacred—their duty toward their fellow-beings. By the way, I have just read of two more failures, one a shoe store and the other a grocery store, and both because of the department store evil! How can small dealers, with only a few hundred dollars behind them, expect to compete with firms whose capitals reach the millions? They are only the poor little fishes in the sea, while the department stores are sharks, sharp-toothed monsters of destruction!"

"I have heard of one department store in Philadelphia, I think, where the proprietor gave situations to a lot of men after he had bought them out or completely ruined their business. That is better than nothing," said Mr. Watkins thoughtfully.

"It is the only recompense possible in such an unjust transaction."

"They do not think it unjust; they call it simply business,'" said Faith bitterly. "The one who sells the most goods is considered the smartest. It is a case where might makes right—the survival of the fittest."

"In other words," replied Mrs. Marvin, "a rich corporation justifies its methods on the grounds that it has a right to transact business on a scale corresponding to its pecuniary ability—there is no question of morality involved. Every man for himself, and the devil take the hindmost. Yet there are people who believe that there is no future punishment for these malefactors."

"God will punish them according to His judgment, mother. It may be here and it may be hereafter. We have nothing to do with their wrongdoing. We must suffer and be brave—that is our duty and our mission."

"And do you see no injustice in that?" cried Mr. Watkins sharply.

"Was it right that poor Mary should be born to poverty and disease and wear her young life out in agony, while so many of the wicked are flourishing? Oh, I have tried not to question or even to think, but the promise of salvation grows daily more dull in my ears. I doubt the mercy of God and I cannot help it!"

CHAPTER XII
A COMPLICATION OF TROUBLES

Faith could think of no words then to comfort Mr. Watkins. His grief was too poignant. She changed the subject.

When he left the house to go home, she put on her hat. There was something she wished to say to him that she could not say before her mother. There was an errand at the grocery that gave her an excuse, and as the hour was not late, Faith welcomed the opportunity.

As soon as they were in the street she told him her experience with the store detective and asked his advice in case she should be annoyed in the future.

Before the words were fairly out of her mouth she wished she had not spoken. There was confusion and shame upon her companion's face, and his lips trembled strangely when he tried to answer her.

For a moment Faith could hardly believe her senses. She stared at him stupidly, while her limbs trembled beneath her.

Instantly a suspicion darted through her brain. She remembered that he, too, had been in the superintendent's office that evening, and that it was possible, even probable, that he knew something about the money.

"Oh, Miss Marvin, this is dreadful!" he managed to say at last. "I did not dream that they would settle upon you! I thought, that is, I hoped, that they had dropped the matter!"

"Then you knew of it," said Faith, her voice sounding faint and far away.

"I knew it, yes," said Mr. Watkins. "In fact, I was sent by Mr. Forbes to stop you, but you had gotten out of the building."

"Is it possible?"

Faith was coming back to her senses now.

"Tell me all you know of the matter, Mr. Watkins," she said, sternly, "and tell me the exact truth. Don't attempt to hide anything!"

Mr. Watkins controlled himself and told her the whole story—how the superintendent had suspected her of stealing the money and sent to have her brought back at once and had been disappointed.

"An hour later," he continued, "he got a telegram from his wife. His son was dying and he had to go home. Since then there had nothing been done about the robbery."

Faith drew a long breath after the young man finished.

"So appearances are against me," she said, with a sigh. "I am at the mercy of a rascal like that detective, Hardy."

Mr. Watkins said nothing, but he was as pale as death. When he tried to comfort her the words nearly choked him.

Faith saw it and pitied him even while she wondered. A few moments later she bade him a cordial "good-night." If there was any suspicion in her heart it did not show in her manner.

She was walking slowly home from the grocery, plunged in the most serious thought, when a well-dressed man of middle age appeared suddenly before her.

"I beg pardon, miss," he said, raising his hat, "but I am a stranger in this neighborhood and am looking for a certain number. If you live about here perhaps you will kindly direct me."

"I will, with pleasure, sir. What number do you wish?" asked Faith.

As she spoke she paused directly in the glare of a gas lamp.

As the light fell on her face the stranger stopped abruptly.

"By Jove! What luck!" he cried, gayly. "The very angel I was thinking of!"

"What do you mean, sir!" cried Faith, who was now thoroughly frightened. "If you wish me to direct you, state the number that you seek at once! I am not in the habit of being addressed by strangers!"

"My dear child, don't get angry. I shall not harm you," said the man, politely, "but you surprised me out of myself. I did not dream of meeting you."

As Faith still stood staring at him he continued, speaking hurriedly, and his manner became so chivalrous that the young girl soon accused herself mentally of rudeness.

"You see, it is this way, miss. I was thinking of the sweetest little girl in the whole big world, and when I saw your face you were so much like her that to save my soul I could not help that exclamation. You will pardon me, I am sure, for I meant no harm whatever! I am old enough to be your father, so you see you have no reason to fear me."

"I spoke hastily," said Faith, slowly. "I had no wish to be rude, but you must admit that I had cause to feel a little startled."

"You did, indeed, and I apologize humbly, but am I not right in thinking that I have seen you somewhere before? Are you not employed in the department store of Denton, Day & Co.?"

Faith looked at him in surprise.

"I have worked there two days," she began, a little hastily.

"And I have seen you twice," replied the stranger, promptly. "Your face is a sweet one. I could not forget it."

The words were spoken so quietly that Faith could not resent them. She was moving slowly toward her home now, feeling a little bit nervous.

"That is a dreadful life for a girl," went on the man, very quietly. "It is agony for the poor things, both of mind and body!"

"You are right, sir," cried Faith, who had thought instantly of Miss Jennings. "The shop girls' life is one continuous drudgery. She is the slave of circumstances and the victim of conditions."

"I am surprised that so many enter the life. There are surely other vocations. They choose the hardest one possible."

"But do they choose?" asked Faith, who had become interested in spite, of herself. "Are they not driven this way or that, according to their opportunities? In my case there was no choice. I had tried everything else. Hard as it is, I am thankful for my present employment."

The man looked at her sharply. There was genuine sympathy in his face. Almost involuntarily he broke out in violent sentences.

"You girls are to blame in great measure for all this, and where the fault is not yours it lies with your parents! Instead of cultivating your graces you bedraggle them with labor! Instead of marketing your smiles you trade in blood and sinew! Every day in that store means a year off of your life; every anxious moment means an inroad into your rightful happiness! Why will you not see the folly of your ways? Why can you not understand that it is a false morality which is killing you? Why, if I were a girl"—his voice had dropped to the most persuasive cadence—"I should value my beauty too highly to hide it behind a counter, and my subsistence should be the boundless reward of affection, rather than the niggardly recompense for wasted tissues! Of course, I shock you, because you have done no thinking for yourself. A lot of narrow souled ancestors have done thinking for you. They have brought you here to let you shift for yourself, but woe to you if you offend one of their petty notions of honor. See, child! I have money, I have constant ease. Could you blame me for offering to share it with youth and beauty?"

As he breathed these words he gazed at Faith eagerly. The soul in the man had vanished. He was dangerously in earnest.

The thrill that flowed through Faith's veins as he spoke was not of fear, for, child that she was, she understood his meaning, and his words stirred the deepest channels of her soul—she was more grieved than shocked at the man's distorted reasoning.

"You are all wrong," she said, sadly. "You cannot understand! There are some things more precious than gold to us, more precious even than comfort or affection. Not for the world would I lose this 'something' which I possess! It is the haven of my soul at the hour of every trial. It is the one solace of my life in the desperate condition that I have reached. You, a man of years, should not argue so wrongfully. It is wicked to place temptations before the young and wretched."

She had regained her composure as she finished speaking, and a tinge of righteous indignation made her voice vibrate strangely.

"Is it wrong to do good?" asked the man, a trifle sullenly. "Surely comfort, ease, health are the best a man can offer. Nature did not create you girls for a life of toil. You were made for love, for homage and adoration. Yet when one offers you these you turn to your nameless 'something' and, like the martyrs of old, suffer torture and death rather than accept what is your due. It is incomprehensible, truly!"

"Hush! Your words are an insult! I will not hear them. It is true that my knowledge of the world is limited, but this much I know: the God of righteousness has placed me here for a purpose, and that purpose is not to play the coward in time of trouble or to prove traitor to the highest, holiest instincts which permeate my being! Working girl I am and may always be, but my lot is a queen's beside what you suggest! God pity the poor women who have not the wisdom to see it."

She was standing before him now like a beautiful statue, one arm uplifted to emphasize her utterances.

"My God! You are superb! Magnificent!" muttered the man involuntarily. "I would give my life to be worthy of such a woman!"

Faith's arm dropped suddenly, and she drew away with a gasp. There was a look in the man's face that frightened her for a moment.

"You have taught me a lesson," he said, almost hoarsely. "I thank you, child, and I bid you good-evening."

"But the number," cried Faith, as he was turning away. "You wished me to direct you to a certain number."

"Never mind it now. I can find it," was the answer.

He was walking swiftly away in the darkness of the street, when a figure approached him from the opposite direction.

The two met directly under the gas lamp where Faith had been standing a moment before, and as they met Faith heard a sharp exclamation.

Her sharp eyes recognized the newcomer at once. It was no other than Bob Hardy, the store detective.

CHAPTER XIII
A HEAVENLY INSPECTOR

When Faith Marvin reached home after her unpleasant interview with the well-dressed stranger, she was in a state of nervousness that nearly bordered upon hysterics. The fact that Bob Hardy was a witness to what she had supposed was a mere accidental meeting gave her an instinctive clue to the identity of the man, and her cheeks flushed with shame as she connected him in her thoughts with that insulting proposition of the detective.

She had tried to compose herself, as usual, before going into her mother's presence, and succeeded so well that when they retired Mrs. Marvin had no suspicion of the interview. Neither did Faith acquaint her with the extraordinary suspicions against Mr. Watkins, which she now felt ashamed to think she had harbored for a second.

She was much troubled in mind about the latter, for while she felt in her heart that Mr. Watkins was innocent she could not help thinking that he, too, was shielding a thief. She wondered if it was because he felt the same on the subject as had his sweetheart, Miss Jennings. She said her prayers quietly and felt more tranquil after. There was a balm in religion for her trusting heart, which she begged with all her soul to share with others.

It was during this hour that she thought of Mr. Forbes, whom she knew was to bury his only son on the morrow. Suddenly the thought flitted through her head that perhaps employees were somewhat to blame for not expressing more sympathy for their employers in all serious matters.

"Perhaps they think us as heartless as we think them," she whispered to herself; then the impulse came over her to write Mr. Forbes a letter.

She rose quietly, so as not to wake her mother, and penned him the note. It came straight from her heart. She told him she was sorry for his sorrow. Early the next morning she went out and mailed it. Little Dick went with her, hobbling along on clumsy crutches. The child had fallen in love with her at once, and, although he often cried for his sister, Faith could always cheer him and change his tears to laughter.

Late in the afternoon she rode down to the undertaker's. She had not become reconciled yet to parting with Miss Jennings.

As she reached the door two women were just leaving; they were Miss Fairbanks, the buyer, and Maggie Brady. Faith was startled for a minute, for she could not understand their interest. Neither one of them had ever shown the faintest liking for the dead girl, but now she noticed with surprise that they had both been crying. "Truly, every cloud has a silver lining," she murmured to herself, "and who knows but what this is the first glimpse of the lining! Oh, I do hope it will soon show itself to poor Mr. Watkins."

The two women had passed her with a mere nod of the head. She opened the door of the establishment and confronted Mr. Watkins.

"Oh, what is it?" she cried, involuntarily, as she saw his face. "Don't, dear Mr. Watkins; don't take it so badly."

Mr. Watkins put his hand on her arm as she spoke. He was so faint and weak that he seemed obliged to lean on something.

"I—I have explained that matter about the money," he whispered, hoarsely. "Hardy will not annoy you any longer. The thief has been discovered."

He looked so wretched that the tears sprang to Faith's eyes.

"I am glad it is explained," she answered, hastily, "but you are ill, Mr. Watkins. You should go home this minute."

"Home—home!" repeated Mr. Watkins in a vacant manner.

Then with a fearful groan of agony he collapsed completely. As he fell to the floor several of the undertaker's clerks rushed forward and lifted him up.

"Another victim of conditions, of greed and avarice," said a voice in Faith's ear.

She turned quickly and recognized Miss Alma Dean, the woman inspector, whose card she had in her pocket.

Without waiting for Faith to answer, the lady went on speaking. The men were laying Mr. Watkins on a sofa not twenty feet away from the body of his dead sweetheart.

"That poor fellow was a picture of health two years ago, before he entered the employ of Denton, Day & Co. I know his mother well; she is a lovely woman, and he has a younger brother who is also in that store, and liable to follow in this poor chap's footsteps. I just came in to look at that poor girl. I want to stamp her face indelibly upon my memory. Thank fortune I am in a position to remedy some of the evils in this world. As Government Inspector I can do considerable, but I must learn the length and breadth of the evil before I am fit to attack it."

Faith listened breathlessly to every word. The proprietor of the place was also listening, and as she finished, he nodded his head as though he quite agreed with her.

Mr. Watkins was rapidly reviving under the kind care bestowed upon him, but before he was fairly alive to his surroundings Miss Dean took Faith's hand and led her out on to the sidewalk.

"They will take him home—they are very kind people," said the lady, sadly, "but now, dear, you and I are confronted with a problem. How are we to prevent the repetition of this horror?"

As Miss Dean asked the question she did not really seem to expect an answer from Faith; it was more like a spoken expression of thoughts that were vexing her, made to one whom she knew was thoroughly sympathetic.

"This is the saddest demonstration of injustice that I have ever witnessed," she went on, slowly, "yet I know it is mild in comparison with others. It lacks the hideousness of exposure, so far as you see. We only know that one more crime has been added to the list, yet the details of that crime have been carefully spared us."

Faith knew that she referred to poor Mary's death, but she could find no words with which to manifest the depth of her sorrow.

"The fear of the law is our only hope, I guess," went on Miss Dean. "They must be forced to comply with certain regulations. Many of the stores are doing so, under no compulsion whatever, but these people seem deaf to everything but the jingle of their dollars."

"But the law cannot change their hearts," muttered Faith, at last, "so the cure that it effects must of necessity be superficial. Oh, if only the fear of the Lord could be instilled into their system. If they could only be made to feel that to Him they are accountable!" She spoke with enthusiasm, her eyes and cheeks brightening.

"You are a good ally," said Miss Dean, watching her, "but, my dear, the day of miracles is ended."

"But with God all things are possible! It would be no miracle for Him! I did not mean to infer that I or any human being could reach their hearts, still our words and our prayers, are they not noble weapons?"

"I am not so sure," said the inspector, gravely. "I think, dear, I am better fitted to experiment on a purely worldly basis. For instance, I have already reported the condition of that cloak-room, the drainage, ventilation and unsuitable location. Then I have mentioned the inadequate fire appliances in the building as well as the long hours you girls are obliged to stand and the short time which you are allowed for luncheon. I think that several of these matters will be changed at once, but there are others which will take longer or which may never be accomplished."

"It will make them very angry, will it not, when they hear of your report? And the alterations will be expensive, especially when it comes to altering the cloak-room."

"Oh, well, we inspectors cannot worry over any personal feelings, my dear. Our duty is to make right all wrong conditions. We are to look after the health of people, not their money. The only question is how to do this in the quickest possible manner."

Faith glanced at her sharply. She was a handsome woman. There was a resolution in her face that commanded instant admiration.

"I am glad to have seen you to-day," Miss Dean said as they reached the corner. "I find my sympathies are more and more enlisted through acquaintance with you girls. Why, I feel that I would like your employers to spend millions in making your labors a little lighter."

She smiled pleasantly as she spoke and offered Faith her hand.

"Good-by, dear," she said brightly, "there's a good time coming."

Faith watched her as she boarded a car—she was so ambitious, so full of vigor and so nobly intentioned.

"If she were only an inspector sent from God, now," she whispered, then a tremor shot over her frame at such a wonderful suggestion.

"Why should I not be an inspector sent from God," she murmured, "to seek out the dark places and let in the light? If it is only a candle flame it will help a little."

She turned abstractedly, almost dazed by her thoughts.

The next instant she was brought almost rudely to her senses. Some one had called her by name. She turned and faced young Denton.

CHAPTER XIV
MR. FORBES TALKS ON RELIGION

About two hours before the meeting of Faith and young Denton, Duncan Forbes returned from burying his son, and sat down disconsolately in the library of his handsome residence.

Although only the junior partner in the firm of Denton, Day & Co., still his interest, together with his salary as superintendent of the establishment, brought him in every year a princely income.

Then there were other investments of a varied nature, all of which had proven more than ordinarily successful, yet now in his hour of sorrow he could feel no atom of thankfulness, and every hour of his busy life seemed to him to have been wasted.

As he sat staring at the fire he could hardly restrain his feelings, for the words "God will punish you" were ringing in his ears even more clearly now than when he first heard them.

He tried to go over the incidents of that morning when a poor applicant in his office had wrought such havoc with his conscience.

He remembered the five hundred dollars of which he had been robbed, and he also recalled vaguely the conversation he had with a woman inspector in the store immediately after. Then came the message regarding his son's condition, then the death chamber, the grave, and now—desolation. The door opened softly and a servant entered. She bore a tray upon which were laid a number of letters.

After she had gone Mr. Forbes rose and looked them over. He did so listlessly. He had no heart for business.

The first three were business letters, referred to him by the firm with a brief note, stating their importance as an apology for the intrusion.

The next two letters were letters of condolence from members of his church. The last was a cheap envelope, neatly sealed and addressed modestly.

This last he turned over and over between his fingers. There was a vague thought in his brain to which he could give neither shape nor utterance.

Could it be possible? He asked the question and then sneered in answer. The thing was incredible, that he, Duncan Forbes, tyrant and slave-driver, should be remembered by his victims, yet the envelope was redolent of sympathetic surprises.

He tore it open finally and glanced at the words. For just a moment the flame of appreciation sprang up within him.

The note was from Faith Marvin, the new packer whom he had employed. She was "sorry for him," she said, "in this hour of his affliction."

He laid it down with a sigh that ended in a groan. His brow darkened as he looked at it. He was aroused and puzzled. The door opened again and his pastor entered. He came unannounced and in a shrinking manner.

Mr. Forbes turned toward him indifferently and held out his hand. He realized that this call was obligatory. He had been paying for it yearly.

As the two men sat down the minister coughed a little, then he folded his hands meekly—his host knew what was coming.

"I trust that you have become reconciled to this separation, dear Brother Forbes," he began solemnly, "and that you can say in your heart 'The Lord giveth and the Lord taketh away; blessed be the name of the Lord.'"

Duncan Forbes did not answer for the space of a minute, during which time his pastor watched him furtively from under his eyebrows.

"My son was my all," he muttered finally. "It is for his sake alone that I have lived and labored—that by the sweat of my brow I have accumulated my fortune."

The minister sighed with unaffected sympathy.

"Yet God in His mercy has taken him from you. He who seeth the end from the beginning knew what was best, dear brother, for your soul's salvation."

"But of what use is my life now?" questioned Mr. Forbes sharply. "I am a broken reed with no ambition to lean upon. A man whose heart has been plucked by its roots from my body. Is there anything in our religion which can solace me, do you think? Is there a recompense for the sufferings of a heartbroken father?"

"There is balm for every wound, Brother Forbes, if we seek it. Others have suffered your loss and been able to find it."

Duncan Forbes sat back in his chair and stared straight before him. The words had brought to his mind unpleasant visions.

In an instant he was back in his store again, where scores of pale-faced, hollow-eyed youths and maidens were moving about. They all had mothers and fathers or some one who loved them, yet, unlike his Jack, they were weighed down by poverty, the millstone of disease was about their necks, and he, Duncan Forbes, was relentlessly grinding the very spirit out of their frail bodies.

He shuddered involuntarily and that brought him back to his senses.

"Religion! what is it?" he asked unpleasantly. "Has it any practical value in the lives of mortals? I have been a church member for forty years, paying my dues in accordance with the terms of that institution and shirking none of its responsibilities. Now, at the hour of sorrow, I find myself facing my grief alone; there is no power in the church that can help me to bear it. What is religion, I say? Is it a mere mummery of speech? I have been religious all my life; now I find nothing in it!"

"The fault is in you," said his caller, gravely.

Both men had risen and stood facing each other.

"You have been too occupied with other things, brother—too busy, you might say, with worldly matters to search for the spirit that pervades what you call 'mummery.' Surely in your love for Jack you appreciate something of the love of Christ for man; in your dealings with men and women you can realize His interest in humanity, and through your wealth you have the power to reap a harvest of good, yet how have you improved these opportunities?"

Mr. Forbes looked surprised, as well he might. They were the first words of a personal application of belief that his ears had listened to since he could remember.

"But religion has no part in worldly affairs," he said sullenly. "To be born for heaven is to be lost for earth; surely we should take each condition in the order that it comes—wealth, position first; prayer and praise hereafter; earth for the body and heaven for the soul; goods and chattels now, faith our stock in trade for the future. This is practical, is it not? This is good, sound reasoning. You are a minister of the Gospel, yet you can't deny it!"

"I can and do!" cried the minister bravely. "A belief that does not shape the life of the believer is not religion! Faith that does not light the path of the present is not the inspiration of Heaven! The Spirit of Christ is an ever-present reagent, neutralizing every rancor of human strife and blending all grief into harmonious concord. Every human act should be weighed in the balance of a man's belief. If he sacrifice divine faith to worldly ambition, he is in need of the chastening rod, and God will surely punish him!"

"You do not preach that from your pulpit, Dr. Villard," he said slowly, "and there is hardly a man in your congregation who does not need it."

Dr. Villard's thin face turned to a sickly pallor. It was a just retribution. He accepted it meekly.

"We ministers are but human," he began, softly.

There was a rap on the door. It came as a welcome interruption.

When Mr. Forbes opened the door he saw his assistant, Mr. Watkins. The young man's face was the color of a corpse, and his hollow eyes were red from weeping.

"I must see you, if only for a minute, sir," he said hastily, then as he caught sight of the visitor a flush spread over his features.

True to his nature, Duncan Forbes scowled heavily for a moment. He would have sent Mr. Watkins away if his guest had not prevented it.

"As you would be done by, Brother Forbes," he whispered quickly.

The next moment he was gone and Mr. Watkins had entered.

CHAPTER XV
A PLAIN TRUTH FROM MR. WATKINS

Duncan Forbes roused himself to hear his second visitor's errand. He knew that it must be something important, yet he felt bored and disinterested.

Business matters were far from his thoughts to-day, yet for forty years they had consumed his entire attention.

Mr. Watkins seemed to be struggling for words—he looked pained and embarrassed. He shifted his hat from one hand to the other, and his thin face reddened and paled alternately.

For the first time in his life Duncan Forbes looked upon his assistant as another man's son—the loved and loving child of another father. It was a queer sensation; he could not get used to it; then came a memory of Jack, and his emotion conquered for the moment.

"You are excited, Watkins; sit down," he said huskily. "Something else has gone wrong at the store, I suppose. Well, let it go; it can wait until to-morrow."

"No, sir, it can't wait!" blurted out Mr. Watkins. "If it could I should not have come, knowing as I did of your dreadful sorrow!"

Again the thrill of surprise shook the man's every fibre. Another of his victims had remembered that it was his day of grief, and the very tones spoke of sympathy for his affliction.

"Well, then, what is it?" He spoke with some of his old sternness. "Speak out, Watkins; you know my habits. I always expect promptness in these errands."

"But this is purely personal, sir!" answered Mr. Watkins, sadly. "I have come to see you about that five hundred dollars that was taken from your desk last Monday morning."

"What of it?" asked Mr. Forbes with much of his old interest returning. He had been too long a slave to money to loose the bondage immediately.

Mr. Watkins was trembling now so that he could hardly speak. In his weak condition of health the recent deluge of trouble was telling upon him.

"She took it, I suppose, that girl that I employed that morning," said Mr. Forbes, trying to hurry matters. "Has anything been done? I told Hardy to look after it."

He picked up Faith's letter again and glanced at it absently. When he saw the name he dropped it as if it had stung him.

A great wave of color purpled his heavy face, and instantly he was the same old tyrant, raging furiously at the creatures whom fate had made his victims.

"See here, Watkins! Here's her letter! Can you believe such deceit! She not only cursed me that morning with her religious cant, but she stole my money as well; now she mocks my sorrow with a letter like that—she is 'sorry' for me! Do you hear, Watkins? She is 'sorry!'"

The great veins were standing out like cords upon his forehead, and he began pacing the floor in a perfect frenzy of anger.

"Tell Hardy to arrest her and have her locked up at once! I'll make an example of her before the whole store! The idea of her daring to write me a letter!"

"But, Mr. Forbes, please listen!" cried Mr. Watkins at last. This injustice to Faith had brought him to his senses. "It was not Miss Marvin who stole the money! She is a good girl, sir, the best I ever knew, and she is sorry for you, sir; if she wasn't she would not say so!"

"But the money!" roared Mr. Forbes. "Who took the money? If it wasn't the girl, why didn't you say so?"

"I couldn't, sir, at first, but I will say it now; but for pity's sake be merciful, sir. The thief was my own poor brother!"

"What! the boy who tends door?" asked Mr. Forbes in great astonishment.

"Yes, sir; poor Sam took it! He stole it for our mother!"

Mr. Forbes stared at him some time before he spoke again.

"And the girl," he asked finally. "Has Hardy been following her?"

"He has indeed," said Mr. Watkins quickly, "but I dare not report his actions; I have no proofs to offer. Hardy would doubtless deny all that she could say of him, for a girl is helpless in the hands of a villain like Hardy."

"I have found him a good detective," said Mr. Forbes, slowly, "but if you knew who took the money why didn't you tell him?"

"How could I, sir?"

Mr. Watkins had begun to tremble again.

"The knowledge of his sin is already killing my mother; if it becomes public she will die. I was waiting for you to come back to business."

"Well, the boy must be punished!" said Mr, Forbes decidedly. "I cannot be accountable for what may follow."

"Do you mean that you will arrest my brother?" cried Mr. Watkins, "when you know that by doing so you will blast his character forever and drive a poor woman to her grave who has never wronged you?"

"The boy should have thought of that," answered Mr. Forbes, grimly. "I deal with my employees, not with their futures or their mothers."

"But if I return the money! See, I have a part of it here!"

Mr. Watkins almost cried with agony as he held out two hundred dollars.

Mr. Forbes took the money and counted it carefully.

"Let's see, Watkins, your salary is twelve dollars a week," he said slowly. "If I deduct five dollars a week to cover the balance of this, it will be just sixty weeks before I could get my money."

"If I could only find the rest," said Mr. Watkins, groaning; "but Sam says he lost it, and I think he tells the truth. If he hadn't lost it he would have given it all to mother."

Mr. Forbes was drumming lightly on a table by his side. It was evident that two emotions were struggling within him.

"Here is the evening paper, sir," said a maid at the door.

Mr. Watkins moved automatically and handed it to his employer.

"Hey! What is this! A death at our store yesterday, Watkins?"

Mr. Forbes had caught sight of a headline half across the paper.

Mr. Watkins bowed; he could not speak. His employer opened the paper and scanned it hastily.

"Ah! That's right! That's right! Gibson is a clever man! He makes the thing sound right before the public! Denton, Day & Co. will pay for Miss Jennings' funeral, yet they say there is no heart, soul nor conscience in a big corporation!"

He almost laughed as he ran his eye down the columns of the paper, and for a moment his manner became almost confidential.

"That's one of the tricks of our trade, Watkins," he said with a chuckle. "We cater to the weaknesses and foibles of the public, and there's nothing that appeals to them like a report of generosity. Of course, they never stop to think that the poor creatures are much better off dead than alive, and that they really have no hold on the sympathies of others. It's a fad among rich people to weep over the poor! Some of them will probably send flowers to the funeral of that woman, and think themselves angels of light for doing it! I tell you, religion is a trade mark in all lines of business, and I've decided in the last few days that that's about all it's good for!"

He laid the paper down with a smile of satisfaction, then turned toward Mr. Watkins to resume the former conversation.

But a look at the young man's face checked the words upon his lips. The scorn in those hollow eyes burned even through his callous nature.

For a moment he saw himself much as his assistant saw him, a man whose greed of gold never reached its limit, even though lives were sacrificed in his service.

He could not speak although he tried to repeatedly, for the glare of his assistant's eye transfixed him like a magnet.

With one hand upon the door, Mr. Watkins paused to answer:

"The papers don't know it all, Mr. Forbes," he whispered shrilly; "or, if they do, they don't dare to tell what they know. If they did they would add that it was the least you could do—to pay for her funeral after your firm has killed her!"

CHAPTER XVI
FAITH'S TALK WITH YOUNG DENTON

"Miss Marvin, I beg that you will excuse this intrusion," said James Denton as he joined her on the street after her call at the undertaker's, "but there is something I wish very particularly to say to you; it is something regarding that poor girl, Miss Jennings."

He had raised his hat politely and stood regarding the young girl in a most courteous manner. As Faith studied his face she could see that he meant no disrespect, but was painfully in earnest.

"I shall be glad to hear anything that you have to say about poor Mary," she answered sadly, "for she was my very dear friend, although our acquaintance was a brief one."

"Let us walk a little, Miss Marvin, please. I can talk better when I'm walking. The fact is, I'm horribly upset, and I don't know why I should be, either."

Faith looked at him sharply. He had removed his hat again and was passing his hand over his brow in a thoughtful manner.

She discovered in that glance that he was a remarkably handsome fellow, for youth, even in its hour of sorrow, cannot help being attracted to all that is gracious and beautiful.

His eyes would have been fine had their glance been a little more steady, but he shifted his gaze constantly, like one who possesses an undecided nature.

"What I have to say is this," he began very bluntly. "I think the firm should arrange to let all you girls attend the funeral of Miss Jennings, and I don't exactly know how to go to work to get them to do it."

"Oh, what a lovely idea!" exclaimed Faith, impulsively, "and it is so kind of you think of it, Mr. Denton," she added.

The young man blushed a little at her enthusiastic words, but went on talking as calmly as possible.

"I've been doing a little thinking since Miss Jennings died; I don't know why, for the death of a clerk doesn't usually affect me."

"Perhaps it was because it occurred in the store," suggested Faith, gently. "You have probably not known the details of any other such sad occurrence."

"That is doubtless it," said Mr. Denton promptly, "but another thing is this: I knew Mr. Watkins before he went to work for my father. His folks used to be rich, you know, and Fred was always a good fellow. He was in love with the girl, and I can't help feeling sorry for him, though, as I said before, I don't quite understand why I'm interested."

"Poor fellow! He needs all our sympathy," cried Faith. "He is lying at the undertaker's now in a terrible condition!"

"Is that so!" exclaimed Mr. Denton. "Why, I met him not more than an hour ago; he was just coming from Mr. Forbes, the superintendent. His face was positively ghastly when I saw him. No doubt old Forbes had been giving him the devil!"

"Surely not at this time!" cried Faith in dismay. "He could not be so cruel—so utterly heartless!"

"Forbes has no heart; he is a machine!" said young Denton. "He is simply a human octopus for pulling in money. Not that I object to money," he added, with a laugh, "but I hate to see men make it through such inhuman methods!"

Faith was utterly astonished at the young man's words. She had been led to believe that he was a thoroughly unscrupulous person, but here he was expressing her own sentiments exactly.

In an instant the young man noticed her look of surprise.

"You are puzzled," he said quickly. "You thought I was nothing but a brainless young scamp! No doubt you have heard my character from the girls in your department!"

"Oh, no!" said Faith quickly. "I have not heard that, indeed! But you will pardon me, Mr. Denton, I did think you were unprincipled, else why should you come in the store and try to make fools of all the young women?"

"Not all of them, only the prettiest!" laughed young Denton, gayly. "Surely a man can flirt a little without doing any harm, and the girls all like it—why shouldn't they, Miss Marvin?"

"But do you ever think what this flirting means?" persisted Faith, who had lost all her timidity and was plunging into the subject in earnest.

"It means a good time and a lot of money spent," said the young fellow, still laughing. "But why not spend it on the girls? Don't they help the governor to make it?"

"Oh, Mr. Denton!" cried Faith, who was now thoroughly shocked. "Is it possible that you are speaking now of your own father?"

"I certainly was," was the unabashed answer. "I did not mean to be disrespectful; that is only a habit."

"A very bad habit," said Faith, reprovingly, "but to return to the subject of poor Mary's funeral. Do you think if we asked for a day we would get it? You know, the store is closed to-day; they might not like to lose another."

"Of course, they wouldn't like it, but that don't make any difference," said young Denton, grandly. "What was Jack Forbes's funeral to you clerks, anyway? The closing to-day was only a bluff—one of the bluffs that all stores put up to keep the good opinion of the public. Now, this affair is entirely different. This girl was one of you, and you ought to be allowed to attend her funeral!"

"Have you spoken to your father?" asked Faith, after a minute.

"Not yet, but I'm going to. Now this is my plan: You get up a petition and get the clerks to sign it and then you go yourself to old Forbes to-morrow. He'll be worse than a brute if he dares to refuse you! Meanwhile I'll see my father at home to-night. He's a little soft on me yet, even if he is a hard-headed old sinner!"

"Oh, Mr. Denton, don't say such things!" cried Faith, "I will never talk to you again if you persist in speaking so of your father!"

The young man threw back his head and had a hearty laugh.

"You're the most innocent little kitten I ever saw," he said softly; "it's a deuced shame that you have to work for a living!"

Faith's eyes blazed angrily before he had hardly spoken the words.

"I am glad to be able to earn my living!" she said sternly; "it is ever so much nobler than to be living on one's parents!"

The flush that mantled the young man's brow showed that her words had struck home, but he tried to turn it off with a neatly put compliment.

"I'm a sad beggar, I know, Miss Marvin, but I'm going to reform! I never wanted to be different until, well, until now—to be honest."

"You are not serious, Mr. Denton; I see laughter in your eyes," said Faith, smiling. "But I will get up the petition at once, as you suggest, and I shall pray that our appeal may not be in vain."

She had paused at a street corner and was extending her hand to say good-by to the young man when a woman passed them and jostled Faith rudely.

It was Maggie Brady, the girl who loved Jim Denton. As she faced them for a second both saw that her eyes gleamed dangerously. Without even stopping she made a remark to Faith—the words were hissed between her teeth with the venom of a serpent.

"You'll be sorry for this, you little hypocrite! I thought you were too pious to be altogether healthy!"

Faith turned as pale as death as the woman strode on; James Denton was smiling in a half-hearted manner.

"That is the result of your flirting," Faith managed to say at last. "Oh, Mr. Denton, can't you see what you've done? You've made that woman love you, and now she is going straight to destruction!"

CHAPTER XVII
THE PARTNERS DO A LITTLE TALKING

Mr. Forbes was at his office in the store early the next morning after his interview with Mr. Watkins. He would have been glad to stay away for another day, but there were many details of the business that needed his attention. Sam Watkins, his office boy, was not waiting for him as usual, but Mr. Forbes was confident that he could find him when he wanted him. He looked around for his assistant, but he was absent also. This fact was more annoying, because it aroused his suspicions.

"Bolted!" he muttered with an angry frown. "Ten to one he's run away and I'll never get my money."

Then he smiled a little, for he knew that Watkins had no funds with which to make his escape, but even if he had there were many ways of catching him.

As he seated himself at his desk both of his partners entered, and there were expressions of condolence offered in a punctilious manner.

"Sometimes I think that we fathers are all wrong," remarked Mr. Denton, after the condolences were over. "We bind ourselves hand and foot in the bondage of business, and all for what—our wives and children! If they needed such a sacrifice we would not begrudge it, but the more they have the more they want, until the head of the family is a mere automaton—a machine to pamper useless folly."

This was a lengthy speech for the senior partner to make, as he was naturally a reticent man, who allowed others to do the talking.

"You may be right," remarked Mr. Day pompously, "still, you must admit that wealth brings advantages even to us who slave—we can drop business cares and go abroad now and then—our time is our own beyond a certain figure."

"I have never reached that figure," said Mr. Forbes, very dryly, "and further, when I drop the reins the horses run wild, for be as careful as you may in the choice of employees there is never one who will not take advantage of your absence—the exceptions are so rare that they are scarcely worth mentioning."

"Well, I for one am getting discouraged," said Mr. Denton. "There's that boy of mine, Jim; how is he repaying my efforts?"

There was no answer to his question, but he did not expect one. After a moment's silence he finished his observations.

"If that boy had a million he would spend it in a month, yet no one has ever yet accused him of being vicious. I've set him up in business and everything else—he's had money and an example, but with it all, what is he?"

"Perhaps you are not strict enough," suggested Mr. Day, who was thanking his stars at that moment that he had no children.

"It will take something besides discipline to make a man of Jim."

Mr. Denton sighed as if he was very unhappy.

"Oh, he'll marry and settle down some day," said Mr. Day, laughing. "When he has a family to support he'll take life more seriously."

"I wish he had one," said Mr. Denton, speaking quickly, "but I hope he'll marry a working girl and not a 'society lady.'"

Both of his partners looked up in unfeigned surprise, but it was evident that the words had been said deliberately.

"There's a girl, a packer, down in the ribbon department. I've only seen her once, but she's a perfect beauty. That's the kind of a girl that would make a good wife; she's not afraid of work and she's honestly religious."

Mr. Forbes and Mr. Day were almost gasping now, but Mr. Denton went right on as though his words were not extraordinary.

"When that Miss Jennings died this girl held her in her arms. She's not over seventeen, yet death did not even frighten her. In that poor girl's last hour she was her only comfort, and if I ever saw an angel I saw one at that moment."

Some one tapped on the door, but no one rose to open it. Mr. Denton waited a moment and then went on with his subject.

"I don't remember how I happened to be in the basement that day. Oh, yes, I do. Mr. Forbes was away, and Mr. Gibson sent for me. I was waylaid on the first floor by one of those Government Inspectors; she went with me to the cloak-room. I simply couldn't stop her! When I got there that girl, Miss Jennings, was dying, and what do you think, with her very last breath she looked me in the face, and said she 'forgave' me."

"What!"

Mr. Day leaned forward with astonishment on his features.

Mr. Forbes half arose from his chair, and then fell back heavily.

Before he spoke again Mr. Denton began pacing the office floor. He was becoming more and more disturbed as he continued his recital.

"They tell me that girl has been with us six years, and that she has never lost a day except from sickness. She was a consumptive always—inherited it from her mother—but in spite of it, she had to work to support herself and a brother. She was getting ten dollars a week at the time she died, yet the cashier tells me that her checks for one hour alone have frequently amounted to twenty dollars. I tell you, this bit of information has set me to thinking, and the outcome of my thoughts is a simple question: 'Are we men or brutes?' That is what I want to know, and as it concerns you two as well as me, I'm going to ask you to answer it!"

There was the silence of death in the superintendent's office. Even Mr. Denton stood perfectly still as he asked his question.

Suddenly Mr. Day raised his head with a little jerk. His cheeks became inflated as he tried to assume his usual bearing.

"It is possible we have been a little thoughtless," he said sweetly, "but our subordinates should attend to these matters; that is what they are paid for."

Mr. Forbes wheeled around in his chair and faced the speaker.

"I have hired no subordinates on that basis," he said distinctly. "My orders have been to get all the work possible out of a clerk, and when they were incompetent or in any way useless, turn them out and get new ones, and I believe that I have acted with the full consent of my partners."

Mr. Day looked crestfallen for about a minute.

"Oh, if you put it that way, why, of course, Mr. Forbes. We could not expect to sell our goods with a lot of dummies behind our counters."

"We've had worse than 'dummies,'" spoke up Mr. Denton. "We've had skeletons and lunatics and almost corpses! Just go down and look at them, men, women and children! There's not ten healthy human beings on any floor in the building; yet they came to us, many of them, glowing with health, like Miss Marvin."

"Are they worse than at other stores?" asked Mr. Day, sullenly.

"I don't know," was the answer; "but that doesn't matter."

"They get their pay regularly," said Mr. Forbes. "Further, we do not solicit their services, nor compel them to stay with us."

"No; we merely take advantage of their wretched conditions to secure their services cheap," said Mr. Denton bitterly; "then instead of bettering their lot we grind them lower and lower, until at last they die either forgiving or cursing us."

There was another silence more oppressive than the first; then Mr. Day rose slowly and started to leave the office.

"We are exciting ourselves foolishly, I think," he said loftily; "neither you nor I, my partners, can hope to remedy the conditions of labor."

He closed the door softly, and was free from the unpleasant atmosphere of the office.

As he did so, a young girl stepped out of the elevator and walked directly to the door which he had just closed behind him. He turned and looked at her—she was as a saint. Almost instinctively it came to him what his partner had said, that she was "not afraid of work and was honestly religious."

"Pshaw! What nonsense!" he muttered. "Think of our patterning after a saint! It is strange how death will upset some men, but they'll get over it when they hear the money jingling!"

He opened the door to his private office just as a boy came upstairs with a message from Mr. Gibson.

"Mr. Watkins was taken to the hospital last night," it read; "are we expected to do anything? There's a reporter from the *Herald*."

"I'll send down the answer in a moment," he said to the boy, "or, wait; tell Mr. Gibson to say that we are looking into the case, and if our employee is found to be deserving he will be cared for by the firm. The reporter can call again if he wishes anything further."

With the note in his hand he went back to the superintendent's office.

CHAPTER XVIII
FAITH BECOMES AN OBJECT OF JEALOUSY

As Mr. Day opened the office door with the message in his hand, he hesitated for a moment, in something like bewilderment.

Faith Marvin was standing before his partners with a paper in her hand, and just as he entered she was speaking eagerly. "We would be so thankful if you would do this, gentlemen—even for half a day, if you cannot spare a whole one. You see, poor Miss Jennings has no family, only a crippled brother, so we clerks are really her brothers and sisters. She was a dear, good girl; so patient and resigned. If we could lay her in the grave ourselves it would be a sweet and solemn pleasure."

She turned from one of the men to the other with her appealing glance, even including Mr. Day as he stood irresolute upon the threshold.

Mr. Forbes was the first to recover his voice. The girl's appearance and the petition had made them both dumb for a minute.

"It can't be done, Miss Marvin," he said, curtly. "It would be establishing a precedent; isn't it so, Mr. Denton?"

"But surely, Mr. Forbes, such a precedent would do no harm!" cried Faith quickly. "Poor Mary is the first clerk who has died in the store, you know. It isn't at all likely that there will be any others."

Mr. Forbes stared at her curiously. He was not exactly angry. As she stood supplicatingly before him, she was radiantly beautiful.

"Why not have it in the evening?" suggested Mr. Denton. He had found his voice at last, and came to the superintendent's rescue.

"The girls are so tired at night," said Faith, sighing. "I thought of that—but it did not seem advisable."

"We might arrange for a few of you to be away on that day. Surely, you were not all Miss Jennings' friends; there is no excuse for the whole store going into mourning."

Mr. Forbes spoke decidedly and with a little of his old crustiness. The spell of the girl's magnetism was beginning to leave him.

"That would mean extra work for the clerks who remained," was Faith's desperate answer, "and poor Mary would be the first to object to that. Their duties are hard enough now. Oh, no, sir; I am sure that would not be thought of for a minute. If there is work to be done, we will all stay and do it, but if you only would relieve us for a few hours, we would be deeply grateful."

"It wouldn't do at all, Mr. Forbes!"

Mr. Day spoke, if anything, more pompously than ever. "Pardon me, but we have lost one day this week. We can't afford another."

"That settles it," said the superintendent, wheeling around in his chair. "You will please return to your duties, Miss Marvin; we cannot allow your petition."

Faith walked slowly from the office with the tears springing to her eyes. Before she reached the ribbon counter a floor walker stepped up to her. She had never seen him before, but recognized him at once as the Mr. Gunning whom she had heard the girls say belonged in that department, but was away just then upon a short vacation.

"You have been gone more than fifteen minutes, No. 411," he said, sharply. "Hurry over to your counter; Miss Fairbanks wishes to see you."

Faith looked at him timidly. He was a silly looking young man who wore a flaming red necktie and curled the ends of his mustache.

"Another tyrant," thought Faith, but she only bowed respectfully. Already in her short term of service she was getting used to tyrants.

"I am going to put you in Miss Jennings' place for a day or two," was the buyer's greeting. "I am short of girls, so you will have to do. Miss Jones will tell you what you don't know about the stock, and I hope you'll be very careful in your measurement of the ribbon."

"I will do my best," said Faith, very sadly. She was soon standing behind the counter, a full-fledged saleswoman. For some reason there had been nothing said about the half day that she had lost, but Faith knew only too well that she would be heavily fined for her absence. Still, it was better than being discharged. She accepted the alternative thankfully.

If Bob Hardy was in the store he kept out of the ribbon department, for Faith looked around for him nervously several times, and was greatly relieved when she did not see him.

Once she overheard two cash girls talking about the robbery in the office, and as they mentioned the name of Watkins she paused involuntarily and listened.

"They say he's got brain fever," said one of the girls. "Well, I'd think he'd be crazy with all that's happened."

"It must be awful," said the other girl. "Why, his brother was only a kid, and, to think, he stole five hundred dollars!"

Faith almost gasped for breath at this information.

She tried to speak to the girl, but her lips and tongue seemed palsied. She understood now what poor Mr. Watkins had suffered, and to think she had distrusted him—even for one brief second!

Several times during the forenoon she saw Maggie Brady watching her, and the hatred in her eyes was too plain for Faith not to see and understand thoroughly.

Her first thought was to see Maggie and explain her conversation with James Denton, but she thought better of it later, and decided to keep silent. Miss Fairbanks was plainly upset and nervous. She scolded the girls constantly, and seemed irritated beyond measure. Whether Mr. Gunning's presence was responsible for this nervousness Faith could not tell, but it was plain that the two were on bad terms with each other.

On the other hand, Mr. Gunning had many friends in the department. Miss Jones smiled at him frequently, as did several of the others.

Faith was standing erect behind her counter when a sharp-looking woman came up. She began asking to see ribbons of various widths and colors. Faith tried to wait upon her as rapidly as possible, but as she was not familiar with the stock, she got sadly muddled.

"How long have you been here?" asked the woman suddenly.

"Only about two hours at this counter," said Faith, sadly. "I am very sorry, but I am afraid I have not waited on you properly."

"Do you mean that you are a new girl altogether?" asked the woman.

Faith glanced up innocently, and saw both Miss Fairbanks and the floorwalker scowling at her.

As quick as their eyes met Miss Fairbanks made a signal. It was as plain as day. Faith was to answer no questions.

The woman was looking at her with her shrewd, sharp eyes.

"Well, why don't you answer?" she asked, half smilingly.

"I was a packer for two days," said Faith very softly. She could see no reason why she should not answer the question.

As the woman moved away from the counter every eye in the department followed her, and Faith noticed how alert all the girls were to wait upon her.

As soon as she disappeared Miss Fairbanks rushed up to Faith.

"What did she ask you?" she questioned breathlessly; "and what did you tell her?"

Faith repeated the conversation in open-eyed wonder. When she had finished Miss Fairbanks breathed a sigh of relief, but her face was still clouded. "I guess they won't blame me for putting in a green girl," she said slowly. "Anyway, there was no one else. I'm awfully short-handed as it is."

"We ain't to blame if they don't give us help enough," remarked Mr. Gunning, savagely. "This firm is too stingy to keep a full force of clerks. Still, if one of them is sick or dies, there's always a row about changes."

"Well, if she feels like it, she'll report, and that will mean trouble," said Miss Fairbanks, sighing; "but perhaps she won't. There are some good-hearted ones among them."

"Who was she?" asked Faith as soon as she got the opportunity.

"Only one of Denton, Day & Co.'s spies," was the answer. "They are better known in the business as 'Private Shoppers.'"

Faith looked aghast at this information.

"Didn't you ever hear of them before?" asked Miss Jones, coming up. "Why, every store has them; they are a part of the system."

"Do explain!" cried Faith; "I am still in the dark. Do you mean that that woman was a regular detective?"

"Oh, Lord, no; she wasn't a detective at all! She's a spy, I tell you, the genuine article! Her principal work is to trot around in other stores and learn all she can about their 'specials' and prices, and get all the information possible in order to keep her employers posted on what their rivals are doing, and besides that she is expected to prowl around this store at irregular intervals, and we are not supposed to know that she isn't a legitimate customer. She asks questions and pumps and finds out all we know; then she makes us take down all our goods and put them all back, just to see if we are in the habit of keeping our tempers. Oh, she can make life miserable for us if she chooses! A bit of indifference on our part, and up a report goes, straight to the superintendent, and we get bally-hoo from the buyer shortly after! I tell you, we've got to be saints to keep our jobs in this place, but once in awhile, when we get the chance we let out on some safe party—that's the way we square ourselves. We can't always be angels."

"I've got a lot to learn," said Faith with a sigh, "but I shall always be civil and attentive to my customers, so I don't think I shall have much to fear from that particular direction." At just that moment a messenger boy came along the aisle. He had come from outside, and was looking for some one.

"Who is it? What do you want?" asked Mr. Gunning, going forward.

"Miss Faith Marvin," said the boy, loudly. "I have a package for her."

Faith looked up in surprise, as she heard the words. She signed the boy's ticket automatically, and accepted the package.

As she did so, a card dropped from under the cord with which it was tied.

Maggie Brady, who was watching her closely, sprang forward and snatched it up in an instant. As she laid it on the counter she fairly trembled with rage.

She had read the words which were written on the card.

They were simply: "To Miss Marvin, with the compliments of Jas. T. Denton."

CHAPTER XIX
FAITH GETS ACQUAINTED WITH THE THIEF

It was impossible for any one to see Maggie Brady's face without reading in it how much she hated the girl who she thought had stolen her lover from her. Miss Fairbanks turned on her heel and walked away laughing, while several of the clerks began jeering Maggie quietly.

"You are not the only pebble on the beach; did you think you were, Mag? There are others, you see! Why, you're not one, two, three in Jim Denton's good graces!"

"Off with the old and on with the new! There's no one proves the truth of that proverb oftener than a certain young man I could mention! However, Maggie, don't throw up the sponge! You've got the first claim on Jim Denton—why don't you let him know it?"

Faith listened to these words in utter amazement. She was distressed beyond measure that this unfortunate thing should have happened.

She was glad enough when a number of customers came in. She was beginning to dread these occasional lulls in business. Maggie Brady had not said a word in reply to any of the taunts, but her face had paled until the two spots of rouge on her cheeks gave her a ghastly look that was positively shocking.

Faith felt so sorry for the girl that she did not know what to do, but there was no time to waste in thinking, for she was being addressed by a customer.

"My dear, can you tell me where that young lady is—Number 89, I think, they called her. She waited on me so nicely the other day that I would like to see her again if there is no objection."

Before she had finished speaking Faith had recognized her. It was the kind old lady whom Miss Jennings had dragged behind the counter during the excitement about the fire. She had said at that time that she would not forget her.

Faith's ready tears had already sprung into her eyes, but she managed to tell the good woman what had happened.

When she finished speaking the lady looked terribly grieved. She could not speak for a moment—she was so shocked and indignant.

"That settles my shopping in this place any more," she said finally. "I will not trade in a store where my sister women are so badly treated."

Faith saw her opportunity, so she hurriedly told her about the petition, and how the house that had closed its doors because a son of the junior partner died would not spare half a day to let its employees attend the funeral of a comrade.

"What a shame!" said the lady, carefully lowering her voice. "What a pity that the public should not know of all these things. I am sure it would result in their losing many customers."

"If there was only some way to make them more considerate," said Faith sadly, "and I am sure there is—I am praying for them daily."

"Dear, dear, you don't say!" said the lady, a little surprised. "Why, it is strange that I did not think of that before, for I am accustomed to going to the Lord with everything!"

"Oh, I am so glad to hear that!" cried Faith impetuously. "Then you will help me to pray for the firm that employs me! It may be that God will touch their hearts. We must do our best and then be patient."

"You are a brave young girl and a wise one," said the lady. "Many who are much older than you have not learned that lesson."

The customers were beginning to push and crowd about the counter, so the old lady went away to allow Faith to wait upon them. As she left the department, Mr. Gunning bowed to her politely.

"One of our best customers," he remarked to Miss Fairbanks as he passed her.

At luncheon time there was none of the usual laughter in the cloak-room. The girls were all thinking of Miss Jennings and talked almost in whispers. In a very few minutes Faith saw a young woman come in. It was the girl who had stolen the piece of jewelry on the day of the fire and for whom Miss Jennings had pleaded so successfully.

When Faith saw her she felt a thrill to the very tips of her fingers. It was a thrill of thankfulness that she had not denied the dead girl's request to show mercy to the poor sinner who had been so wronged by her parents.

As soon as she could she walked over and stood by the girl. She was a sallow brunette but her features were regular and delicate.

"Do you mind my talking to you a little?" Faith asked softly. "You see, I know almost no one in the store except Miss Jennings, and now that she is gone I am very lonely."

"Why, no, I don't mind your talking to me, why should I? I guess it ain't necessary to wait for an introduction. Got anything in particular you want to say to me?"

The girl's answer was prompt, but not at all unpleasant.

"Oh, no; that is, not now," said Faith very quickly. "I just want to get acquainted. You know I could see you plainly when I was a packer and, well, I liked your looks and that's about all there is to it."

While she was speaking, Faith was conscious of a change in the girl's face. She was evidently trying to read her to see if there was anything behind this desire for an acquaintance.

Faith tried to smile brightly as she looked into her eyes. She knew that she must win this girl's friendship if she wished to help her.

"Let's sit down here," said the young woman shortly. "I like this corner; it's lighter than the others."

They both sat down and opened their baskets, and while they hurriedly swallowed their luncheon, they talked a little.

"My name is Faith Marvin and I have Miss Jennings' place at present at the ribbon counter. I wrote that petition that you signed this morning. Isn't it too bad that the firm will not grant us that sacred privilege of accompanying our dead friend to her last resting place?"

Faith had introduced herself as well as she could, and now waited for her companion to follow her example.

"My name is Lou Willis and I hate funerals," said the girl. "I can't see why in the world you ever wrote that petition."

The words startled Faith; they were so sharp and unfeeling.

"Why—you signed the petition," she said after a minute.

"Oh, of course I signed it, but can't you see why, you ninny? If we get a day off I'll go somewhere on a lark! You don't catch this chicken attending any funerals."

Faith was so shocked this time that she could not speak, but the girl rattled on without apparently noticing it.

"I'm not one of your milk and water Sunday school girls! If I ever get religious at all I'll join the Salvation Army! Do you know that's a great scheme, that Salvation Army? You get six dollars a week and your husband picked out for you. Really, that's a great inducement, Marvin, when you come to think of it! I'd never be able to pick out a husband myself. I'm what they call too—too—oh—you know—fickle!"

Faith forgot to eat, she was so astonished. This was a type of woman that she had never dreamed of. Was she joking or serious? Faith could not decide. As she sat pondering and staring, her companion went on talking calmly.

"That Maggie Brady has it in for you, they tell me—but say, for goodness sake, how did you manage to cut her out with Jim Denton? Why, he's been sweet on Mag for at least three months, and that's a long time for Jim. I really began to think he was serious."

She paused to take a mouthful of bread and butter, so Faith attempted to speak. The words came slowly, for she was a little uncertain how to say them. "I am sorry if Miss Brady does not like me, I am sure. But you are wrong, Miss Willis. I have not 'cut her out' with Mr. Denton. On the contrary, I have never spoken to the young man but once, and that was yesterday, when he suggested that I write that petition."

"But he sent you a package to-day," said the girl, staring. "He must be badly smitten to be sending presents in such a hurry."

"It was only a box of candy," said Faith, hastily. "I gave it to one of the cash girls. I don't understand what made him send it."

"You must be silly if you don't," said the girl, laughing harshly.

At just that instant Maggie Brady passed close by them, and Miss Willis seeing her, raised her voice a little.

"Why, he is in love with you, of course," she said, with one eye on Maggie. "If he wasn't he wouldn't be sending you boxes of candy."

"Hush!" cried Faith. "You are cruel! How could you, Miss Willis!"

For answer the girl broke into peals of laughter.

"Oh, I just love Mag Brady—that's why I said it I Can't you see for yourself how much I love her?"

CHAPTER XX
ANOTHER TALK WITH JAMES DENTON

Poor Faith was driven to desperation now. Here was a situation far beyond her wisdom.

That the girl was a petty thief amounted to almost nothing beside her viciousness and animosity toward her fellow beings.

Faith was sorely puzzled over what to say, and while she was trying to collect her scattered wits Miss Willis poured out a little more of her venom.

"If there's a girl in this place I hate it's Mag Brady," she said candidly, "and she knows it, you bet! I haven't tried to conceal it! I'm different from Mag, I hit straight out from the shoulder! She's a sneak and a coward; she'll wait till it's dark before she fights you! You see you haven't been out in the world long enough to read people yet, but I have, I'm a regular veteran in the army of evil."

She laughed loudly as she finished, as though her words were highly amusing. To be experienced in the ways of evil seemed to her to be the highest possible recommendation.

"I hope I shall never know any more about sin than I do now," said Faith soberly, "but really, I seem to be learning more and more every day."

"It won't hurt you," responded her companion patronizingly. "You've got to hold your own, you know; if you don't you go to the bottom. The world is full of sharks and so is this store. The sooner you find it out the better it will be for you."

Faith saw that the girl was growing serious now. What she said was intended to be for Faith's good; whether it was good advice or not, it was the best she had to offer.

"Hello!" cried Miss Willis suddenly. "Do my eyes deceive me, or is that really a plumber that I see over in that corner?"

She raised her voice so that every one heard her, and a clerk in the opposite corner made haste to answer her:

"That's what it is all right, Lou, a real, live plumber! The Board of Health has come to its senses at last, and, thanks to that Government Inspector, we are going to have some 'modern improvements.'"

"I hope we'll have basins enough to go around," cried another voice, "and perhaps there'll be an occasional glimpse of a really clean towel."

"Oh, you mustn't expect too much," answered the plumber, laughing. "I only got orders to do a little puttering. It's just a bluff they are chucking; it won't cost them much if nothin'."

"Which means that you can't get rich all at once!" cried Miss Willis, grinning. "Well, I'm sorry you can't squeeze a fairly good sum out of our nice, generous employers."

Faith went back to her counter, feeling sad at heart. She was beginning to question the wisdom of her mercy toward Miss Willis.

"I don't believe that anything would ever change her heart," she whispered to herself, and then a great wave of shame swept over her as she felt that she had questioned the power of the Almighty.

She stepped behind the counter just in time to see Miss Fairbanks changing the prices on a lot of special ribbons, but before she could ask any questions Miss Jones came up to her.

"There's a milliner in this block who is selling those same ribbons for fifty cents a yard," she said, "and of course, Denton, Day & Co. are not going to stand that; they are going to undercut her in everything until they break up her business. You see, if we sell them for thirty-nine cents, she'll have to come down, which will mean that she'll lose a whole lot of money."

"But won't Denton, Day & Co. be losing money, too?" asked Faith. She was a little too green to quite see the logic of this action.

"Not a cent," was the somewhat surprising answer. "You see, they buy in such large quantities that they get it cheaper than she does; but even if they didn't, they could still make it up on some other goods, while she, poor soul, has no way of squaring her losses."

Faith's eyes opened wide as she listened to this explanation.

"That is exactly what they did with my father," she said slowly. "They undercut his prices so that he could not sell his books, then when his bills came due he could not pay them. Oh, the thing is perfectly horrible, Miss Jones! That poor, poor milliner! Oh, how I pity her!"

Miss Jones had listened with considerable surprise. It was the first she had heard of Faith's personal grievance against the company.

Things moved along quietly after that, and Faith was kept very busy, but through the whole afternoon she was thinking of that ribbon. Every time a roll of it was sold a weight seemed added to her burdens. When she was obliged to sell it herself she felt that she was personally perpetrating a wrong on the milliner.

It was a terrible day, taken altogether, for so much misery and anxiety were crowded into it that she felt ten years older when the gong sounded for closing.

"Can you tell me what hospital Mr. Watkins was taken to, dear?" she asked of one of the little cash girls whom she had heard talking in the morning.

"Don't know," said the child. "I didn't hear. But he's pretty near dead, I guess, and his brother is a thief. He—"

"Hush, child!" cried Faith, quickly. "Don't talk about that, please! It can't do any good, and—and perhaps some one has been mistaken! It's better to say nothing! until one knows for sure. Poor Mr. Watkins! He is indeed in sore trouble!"

"Mr. Watkins is resting very comfortably, Miss Marvin," said a voice just behind her. She turned around quickly and confronted young Denton.

"Oh, have you seen him?" asked Faith, in genuine delight.

"I just dropped in at the office; they wouldn't let me see him," was the answer; "but I learned that there was a chance for him—he was what they call 'comfortable.'"

"I am glad to hear that," said Faith, moving slowly away. They had been standing at the head of the stairs which led down to the cloak-room, and she expected every minute that Maggie Brady would see them.

"Don't go just yet, Miss Marvin," urged Mr. Denton, hastily. "I've just arranged about that funeral; it is to be to-morrow evening."

"Where?" asked Faith softly.

"At the undertaker's," was the answer. "He has a private room for just such purposes. He will bury her the next morning."

"That will be better than I thought," said Faith, very slowly. "I will tell all the girls I know and ask them to tell the others."

"Here's the programme or whatever you choose to call it," said Mr. Denton, sneering a little. "The firm got ahead of us this time, Miss Marvin."

He held out an evening paper as he spoke so that Faith could see it.

With a cry of horror the young girl read the headline. It was a regular "scare head," reaching across two full columns: "Denton, Day & Co.'s Generosity to an Employee!" "A Poor Girl's Funeral That Will Cost the Firm a Large Sum of Money!"

"How's that for hypocrisy?" asked the young man, still sneering. "I say, Miss Marvin, how would you like to be the child of such a father?"

For the first time in her life Faith could not rebuke disrespect. In spite of herself she could not help sympathizing with the sentiments of the young fellow.

"Oh, it is terrible!" she whispered in a heart-broken voice. "Poor Miss Jennings would rather have been buried in 'Potter's Field,' I really believe, than under such conditions!"

"Well, I'm mighty disgusted," said young Denton, bitterly, "although I'm sure I don't know what's got into me to care about it!"

"I guess you never knew just how you felt before," said Faith sweetly. "Sometimes it takes a shock of some kind to bring us to our senses."

"Well, I'm shocked all right," said young Denton, quickly. "Why, when dad told me about that dying girl saying so distinctly that she forgave him, it went through me like a knife! Cut me up worse, I believe, than it did the Governor!"

"Did it really disturb your father?" asked Faith, very eagerly.

"I should say it did!" remarked Mr. Denton, soberly. "Why, the man can't eat nor sleep! I believe her spirit is haunting him!"

CHAPTER XXI
A CHANGE IN MR. DENTON

"Well, Hardy what have you found out about the Watkins family? Something satisfactory, I hope!"

Mr. Forbes spoke to the detective with unusual good nature.

But Hardy closed the office door and advanced to the desk where the superintendent was sitting.

"On the contrary, sir; I have found things very unsatisfactory," was his answer. "Watkins is in the hospital, half dead from brain fever, his mother is a feeble old woman without a penny, and as for that young scamp who stole your money, he's among the missing—he's vamoosed entirely!"

"Well, why don't you find him?" asked Mr. Forbes, a little less pleasantly. "That's what I told you to do! Didn't you understand my orders?"

"I haven't had time to find him," muttered the detective, sullenly. "He's been spirited away. I think he's out of the city."

"So you see no way of getting back that three hundred dollars. Well, there's got to be a way! We can't afford to lose it!"

"Lose what?" asked Mr. Denton, coming in just then.

Mr. Forbes hastily repeated the detective's information.

"You say the mother is penniless and young Watkins critically ill? Well, I should think that was trouble enough for one family," said Mr. Denton slowly. "Mr. Forbes, it is my wish that you should stop right here! I wish you to drop the matter of the money completely."

"What!"

Mr. Forbes wheeled around in his chair and stared at his partner.

"I mean it," said Mr, Denton, "and, what is more, I command it! As senior partner of this firm I expect my orders to be respected!"

Mr. Forbes made a heroic effort at self-control. When he could trust his voice he attempted to answer.

"Perhaps you have forgotten, Mr. Denton, that we are drawing on our funds very heavily this week. There are those alterations in the basement to satisfy the Board of Health and two hundred dollars for that Miss Jennings' funeral. Neither of these expenses would have been incurred if I had not been absent so much of late; but is it wise, do you think, to add to these the three hundred that Sam Watkins robbed us of?"

Mr. Denton seemed to ignore the last half of the sentence. His mind was dwelling upon the other things mentioned.

"What I have not forgotten, Mr. Forbes, is this," he said, quietly: "That funeral that you speak of has given us one of the biggest free 'ads.' that this firm has ever enjoyed. Why, the space it occupies in one paper alone is worth at least a thousand dollars! And, so far as the alterations are concerned—well, I have just ordered them stopped. I'm going to close up that room to employees altogether!"

If the sky had fallen Mr. Forbes could not have been any more surprised. Even the hardened detective almost gasped in astonishment.

"But you have no right to do this," growled Mr. Forbes. "You should consult your partners in such matters, Mr. Denton."

Mr. Denton smiled grimly at the angry man's words.

"You are partners, nominally, yes," he said slowly, "but I hardly think it would pay either you or Mr. Day to oppose me."

His words were very true, as Mr. Forbes well knew. Both he and Mr. Day were deeply indebted to their senior partner. He "owned them body and soul," as many persons would express it.

"I have been doing a lot of thinking in the past two days, Mr. Forbes," went on Mr. Denton, "but as you would hardly appreciate my sentiments, I will keep my thoughts to myself a little longer. Here, Hardy, you are excused from the Watkins affair! Go back to your duties in the store, and see that you are very careful not to annoy any innocent persons."

Bob Hardy made his way out of the office almost in a daze. He had been in the service of the store ever since it was opened, but such instructions as these meant a brand-new departure.

"I wonder what the deuce has got into him, anyway," he muttered. "He talks like a man that's got struck with religion!"

As he walked slowly down the stairs to the first floor of the building he met a brother detective, who stared at him curiously.

"What's the matter, Hardy? Look's if you'd had a shock! Been havin' a set-to with old Forbes, I'll bet a dollar!"

"You're wrong," was Hardy's answer. "It was the old man this time. There's something wrong with the boss. I think he's getting religion!"

"Get out! You don't mean it!" said the other fellow, contemptuously.

"Don't I?" said Hardy. "Well, you just listen to this!"

He repeated the conversation that had just taken place in the superintendent's office.

"Whew! That does sound like it!" said his companion, whose name was Ben Tyler. "He's off his trolley completely, especially about the money!"

"Well, that makes two trow-downs I've got this week," said Hardy, sourly, "but I got the fifty from that masher that I was telling you about! You remember, the swell that calls himself Captain Deering?"

"Yes, I remember," laughed Tyler. "So he caught his bird, did he, or, rather, you caught her for him!"

"I guess it worked all right," said Hardy, slowly. "He met her and talked with her, and that's usually enough. Still, he was glum as an oyster when he gave me the money."

"Mr. Hardy," called a voice at the foot of the stairs. "Come down, quick; you are wanted! There's a shop-lifter over in the hosiery department!"

Mr. Hardy stopped long enough to hear the words, then he made his way directly to the department mentioned.

He paused at the counter and began examining some goods, and as he did so one of the clerks came up to him as though she expected to wait on him.

"Is this the one?" muttered the detective under his breath, at the same time making a slight motion toward the woman.

"Can't say," whispered the clerk. "I just missed the goods. There were six pairs of hose—they all went together."

Hardy glanced again at the woman, whose face was drawn and haggard. She was by far the poorest customer at the counter.

"'Taint's no use tacklin' them others," he whispered to the clerk, "for if I ever nabbed a rich one she'd make things lively for me—but I guess it's the poor one that's got 'em, anyway."

"She looks desperate," answered the clerk, leaning over the counter. "And, you know, she could sell 'em and make a little something."

Hardy nodded knowingly, with his keen glance still on the woman. As she moved slowly away from the counter he followed her at a distance.

Five minutes later she had reached the ribbon department. As she stopped at the counter Faith went forward to wait on her.

"I would like a yard of white ribbon, miss," said the poor woman timidly. "This cheap ribbon, please, for I haven't much money. It's to go on the shroud of a poor dead neighbor."

Faith measured the ribbon quickly and made out a check. As she turned for the woman's money she smiled at her pleasantly.

The next moment Bob Hardy stepped forward and tapped the woman on the shoulder.

"You are wanted in the office, madam," he said, very rudely. "You've been stealing goods in the store, and have got them in your pocket!"

With a cry of terror the poor woman looked up into his face.

"It is false!" she cried wildly. "I never stole a penny's worth in my life! Oh, miss, don't let him touch me! I'm an honest woman!"

In a second Faith darted from her place behind the counter. When she reached the aisle she threw her arms around the woman.

"Stand back, Bob Hardy! Don't you dare to touch her!" she cried, sharply. "Are you so blinded with wickedness that you can't see she is honest?"

CHAPTER XXII
THE BEGINNING OF THE HARVEST

As Faith wrapped her arms around the woman Mr. Denton appeared in the department. He was just in time to hear her ringing question.

There were a dozen or more customers standing around the counters, and they all stood staring in wide-eyed astonishment.

Mr. Denton saw that something must be done at once. It would never do to have a scene like this in the store, for, besides stopping business, it was productive of mischief.

In an instant he realized that he had to deal with Faith, for the woman was clinging to the girl and imploring her protection.

He went forward at once and spoke as calmly as possible.

"Take her up to the office, Miss Marvin, and quiet her if you can. She shall not be harmed. I have no doubt she is innocent."

"And I know she isn't," blurted out Hardy, angrily. He was frantic to think that the woman might escape him.

"Well, whether she is or not, she will be treated kindly," said Mr. Denton. "So use your power to make her go quietly, Miss Marvin."

As he said these words he looked straight at Faith, and the thankfulness in her eyes repaid him in an instant.

"Come, my friend," she said sweetly. "Come with me to the office. There is nothing to be afraid of. You will only have to prove your innocence."

The woman checked her sobs and went willingly. Faith's manner had calmed her fears in great measure. Mr. Hardy followed them to make his accusations, and Mr. Denton led them all to his own private office. As soon as they were there a woman detective was sent for, and the supposed shoplifter was taken behind a screen and searched thoroughly.

While this was being done Faith was bursting with indignation.

"Just think of an innocent person being subjected to such an outrage!" she cried. "Oh, Mr. Denton, is there not some other way to do this?"

"I wish there was," said that gentleman shortly, "for our detective's mistakes have already cost us several thousand dollars."

"I don't wonder," said Faith. "A woman could hardly forgive such an insult, but your detective is capable of far worse, Mr. Denton; he is a very wicked man. I think it is my duty to denounce him."

If a thunder-bolt had fallen at his feet Hardy could hardly have been more astonished. He had not dreamed that the timid girl would dare tell what he had done, particularly as she had acquiesced, as he supposed, in his vile suggestion.

Mr. Denton glanced at her sharply, but she did not quail, although her cheeks were scarlet over the unpleasant remembrance.

"Eh! What has Hardy done? Tell me at once, Miss Marvin. You will never have a better time than when he is present to hear you."

"Oh, I would never tell it behind his back," said Faith. "I always deal fairly and squarely, even with my enemies."

As she spoke, she looked Hardy steadily in the eye. He saw that she would treat him justly, but with no mercy. It was a difficult matter for Faith to tell her tale, but she did it in a way that was absolutely convincing.

"And, oh, Mr. Denton," she cried in conclusion, "is it not enough that we girls have to work so hard without being subjected to such vile, unspeakable horrors?"

Mr. Denton put his hands to his temples and pressed them hard for a moment. The girl's words had overwhelmed him with the full sense of his negligence.

To be able to prevent all or many of these evils and then to be indifferent, thoughtless, neglectful. It had all come to him at once—while the girl was speaking, just as the first tinge of remorse had come when Miss Jennings was dying.

Hardy was standing like a statue, his face purple with anger. It was useless for him to speak. He was convicted without evidence.

Mr. Denton had not replied when the poor woman was led out. She had been searched thoroughly by the woman detective, but there were no stolen goods about her.

"That settles it, Hardy. You can go," said Mr. Denton wearily. "The cashier will pay you. I am done with your services."

"Oh no!"

Faith gave utterance to a pitiful cry. Hardy turned and glared at her a second and then left the office.

"Oh, I did not mean to get him discharged," groaned Faith. "Perhaps a little more mercy would have been far better."

"He deserves no mercy," said Mr. Denton, shortly. There was a decision in his words that was quite contrary to his nature.

The poor woman slipped away thankfully with a grateful smile at Faith, and she was left alone with Mr. Denton. It was the moment she had been praying for, and Faith did not intend to lose it Without a moment's hesitation she spoke softly to her employer.

"Please, Mr. Denton, may I say a few words more? They are not busy downstairs. I am sure they'll not need me."

"Say what you wish," was the answer, and Faith hurried on. Her very soul was on her lips as the words fell from them.

"There are so many things that might be done to improve the conditions for the girls—so much that would add to their happiness and comfort! And it would not take a penny from their sales, either, sir, for surely a clerk that is well and satisfied with her surroundings will be far more courteous to her customers as well as more loyal to her employers. If they could only sit down and rest now and then! It is awful to stand so many long hours. We grow faint and sick, and our backs ache terribly. Why, I have only been in the store a few days, yet last night I could not sleep, I was so lame and weary."

She paused for breath, and then hurried on. Mr. Denton had turned his face away, but was listening intently.

"There are all sorts and kinds of girls in the store, Mr. Denton; some are good and pure, while others are reckless and even vicious. Poor things, they have nothing behind them but memories of sorrow, and there is nothing ahead of them but hard work and trouble. It seems to me God never meant us to have it so hard—if He had He would have made our nerves and our muscles stronger. I think he meant us to do our share of work in the world, but he made men to protect us from the real drudgery of life, whether they were our fathers, brothers, husbands or employers. Of course, I am only a child in years, but it has all been forced upon me by a single week in the store. I have seen more sorrow in three days than I ever dreamed of, and I am praying night and day to be able to relieve it."

She came to a dead stop with the tears choking her voice. The next instant Mr. Denton rose and patted her on the shoulder.

"Bless you, child, you have shown me my duty at last!" he said, hoarsely. "I have neglected it long enough, but, with the help of God, I will neglect it no longer."

Faith gave a cry of joy as she heard the words.

"Oh, my prayers have been answered, dear Mr. Denton!" she cried. "I have been begging God to let me be His torch-bearer on earth, to carry the light into the dark places where it is so much needed, to banish with its glow all the shadows of evil!"

As the last note died away several of the girls burst out crying, and Mr. Denton raised his head and looked at her.

Faith took her seat calmly. The inspiration had not left her. She felt lifted up in soul into a higher atmosphere, where there was no pain or sorrow—only tenderness and rejoicing.

The rest followed swiftly. The last farewell to the departed; with poor Dick moaning and sobbing, the ladies turned their footsteps homeward.

Faith caught a glimpse of Mr. Denton walking rapidly down the street. The next moment she heard her name spoken, and turned to greet Miss Dean, the store inspector.

"Am I too late?" asked Miss Dean, extending her hand cordially. "I was detained at the last moment. I intended being present at the funeral."

"I am sorry you were not," said Faith sincerely, then, after introducing her mother and little Dick, she made an eager communication.

"I really believe, Miss Dean, that poor Mary's death has accomplished great things! I am sure that Mr. Denton has felt it keenly, and that her dying words have awakened his sleeping conscience."

Miss Dean looked surprised, but did not reply, so Faith went on to tell why she thought so.

After she had related her conversation with Mr. Denton in the morning, the lady suddenly put her hand on her arm and looked at her searchingly.

"If you have accomplished that, you have indeed worked a miracle," she said, decidedly; "but deeds speak louder than words. We shall see how Mr. Denton puts his conversation into practice."

"Oh, that's it," said Mrs. Marvin, quickly. "Practice and precept are quite different things. Why, those men are all church members, do you know, Miss Dean; yet see how little their religion is allowed to influence their lives. It seems as if it was kept only for funerals and Sundays."

"That has been my observation in nearly every instance," said Miss Dean, slowly. "I have often said that if I could see a conscientious Christian I would be willing to give up some of my present theories."

"Do tell us one of your theories," said Mrs. Marvin. "I, too, am very bitter against hypocrisy in the church. I shall be glad if some one else feels the same as I do, for my daughter is constantly reproving me for my distrust and bitterness."

"Well, for one thing," said Miss Dean, "I think religion impracticable. No person can follow Christ and succeed in any line of business."

"I agree with you," exclaimed Mrs. Marvin, promptly. "The principles of Christianity oppose success at every turn. To be Christ-like one must always be poor, always weak and, consequently, always downtrodden."

"Your daughter does not believe that," said Miss Dean, smiling.

Faith was so in earnest when she answered that she stopped on the sidewalk and faced them.

"Is there any success greater than this," she asked, eagerly, "to earn those precious words from the lips of our Saviour, 'Well done, thou good and faithful servant,' and to receive at the end of life that joy everlasting that is promised to those who follow Him, even though they bear the cross of worldly failure?"

Miss Dean stared at the young girl in honest admiration. While she questioned her reasoning, she almost envied her. If a simple faith was so satisfying it was certainly worth having, but to natures like hers this simple faith was impossible.

CHAPTER XXIV
MR. DENTON'S ULTIMATUM

When Mr. Denton left that scene of sorrow in which Faith Marvin had just played so sweet a role, he could not possibly have described his tumultuous feelings. Not a night since that sad death in the cloak-room had he been able to sleep peacefully, and even by day his thoughts were sorely disturbed. It was, as his son had said, as though the spirit of Miss Jennings was haunting him.

He was not a bad-hearted man by any means, but, like hundreds of others, he thought only of his own interests and those of his wife and son, who were very dear to him. Out of his own station in life he rarely looked, and the question of equal rights never presented itself to him seriously.

Now, however, something had taken possession of him which he could not understand. He was beginning to meditate upon the rights of others.

As he hurried home after those brief moments at the undertaker's, he went over the scenes of the last few days, trying to determine the causes which led to his perturbation of spirit.

First and foremost in his mind was the conversation with the Government Inspector just before the death of Miss Jennings. She had taken him seriously to task about the condition of the store, and her words had stung him; they were so earnest and truthful. At the very moment of his entrance to the cloak-room he was mentally censuring himself for his almost criminal thoughtlessness for the consideration of others.

Then came the dying words and the glance of those death-glazed eyes. He shuddered even now when he recalled them so vividly.

Since then the awakening of his conscience had come, he had seen himself exactly as he was, a traitor to himself, to humanity, and to his God, and the sight filled him with remorse. He was shamed and repentant.

What to do next, was the question of his soul. He could not undo the past, but, thank God, there was still a present and a future!

He paced the floor of his library long after his wife and son were in bed, but the next morning at breakfast he told them his decision.

Mrs. Denton was a vain woman, who thought of little but the fashions, and whose time was nearly always taken up with what she termed her "social obligations."

Her husband's serious words had the effect of frightening her badly. She looked at him anxiously, as though she feared he had gone crazy.

With young Denton it was different. He was thoroughly astonished and amazed. It was the first time in his life that he had ever heard a word from his father's lips that was not freighted with the so-called wisdom of worldliness.

"I have been blind to my duties and opportunities at the store," said Mr. Denton, in conclusion. "I have been too much occupied with the making and saving of money to bestow a thought upon the higher duties that lay directly in my path—the aiding and protecting of my fellow beings."

"Well, you'll have your hands full, dad, if you help them all," said young Denton when he had recovered a little from his surprise. "I think you ought to do many things differently, of course, but you'll bankrupt yourself if you shoulder all their burdens."

His father did not answer. He was thinking seriously. An hour later he was at the field of action, filled with the righteous determination to do his duty.

Mr. Day sat in his office when his partner entered. He was busy with one of the "buyers," so Mr. Denton stood still and listened.

A large pile of "ready-made" garments lay upon a convenient table, and as the buyer talked, he held them up for examination.

"I find I can get this grade of goods from a man named Finckelstein for ten cents less per garment than I have been getting them from Goldberg. They are very well made, and the quality is satisfactory. No one will ever guess that they are not exactly what we advertise. I ordered this lot for closer inspection. If they are satisfactory to you, sir, I will give him a stock order."

Mr. Day mused a little before he replied. Meanwhile he was fingering the garments in a critical manner.

"Umph! Isn't there a peculiar odor about these garments, Smith?" he asked, after a minute. "I am sure there is! Really, I wish you hadn't brought them in here!"

"I will take them away immediately, sir," said the buyer, apologetically. "They were made in a 'sweatshop,' you see, so it is quite possible they are permeated with unpleasant odors, but I will have them aired before they are put on the counters."

"Are you sure they are not permeated with disease?" asked Mr. Denton, suddenly. "I am told that those 'sweat-shops' are disgustingly dirty places."

"Oh, the Board of Health looks after that," said the buyer quickly, "and, besides, I saw a good many of Finckelstein's hands—they were mostly clean, respectable looking women."

"How much do they get apiece for these?" questioned Mr. Denton again, as he picked up a garment and held it at arm's length to inspect it.

"Oh, about forty cents, I guess; and they can make two in a day. There's a good deal of work on them," was the buyer's answer.

"What do they cost us?"

The question was asked rather sharply.

Mr. Smith consulted his notebook before he answered.

"Fifty cents in gross lots, and sixty by the dozen. We use a great many; it will ruin Goldberg to lose us."

"And what do we get for them?"

Mr. Denton was reaching for the price tag now. His brow was almost black as he asked the question.

Mr. Smith looked at him anxiously—he could not quite comprehend him.

"Two dollars, sir," he answered, smiling—"and they sell like hot cakes. It's the grade of goods that yields us the best profit."

Mr. Denton dropped the garment with a look of horror in his face.

"Take the things away," he said shortly, "and, see here, Smith, don't order any more goods from any of those 'sweat-shops!' I won't have another dollar's worth of them in the building!"

The buyer looked amazed, while Mr. Day turned almost purple.

"We make an average of three hundred per cent on every garment, and we have contracts with some 'sweat-shops' or other for a dozen grades of clothing!"

"We'll buy them off them at a good round sum; then you hear what I say—no more 'sweat-shops,' Mr. Smith!" was the calm reply.

The buyer bundled up his goods and hurried out of the office. His employer's decision nearly took his breath away.

"Are you crazy, Denton?" cried Mr. Day, as soon as the door was closed. "Is it possible that you have lost your senses completely?"

"On the contrary, Mr. Day," was the serious answer. "The truth is, I have only just come to my senses."

He went over and put his finger on an electric button.

"Tell Mr. Forbes to come in here," he said to the boy who answered, then he drew three chairs close together, and sat down in one of them.

When Mr. Forbes entered the office it was very plain that he was angry. His features were darkened by a frown that was, to say the least, forbidding. Without even noticing his expression Mr. Denton offered him a chair and then started in to make some astonishing statements.

"Gentlemen," he said, distinctly, "I have a confession to make. I have already made it to my God, and to my family; it is now fitting and necessary that I make it to my partners. To be as brief as possible, my confession is this: While I have succeeded admirably in laying up treasure on earth, I have woefully failed in laying up treasure in heaven. While I have done my duty from a worldly point of view, by my wife and family, I have been persistently injuring many hundreds of my fellow beings, and showing no consideration whatever for their moral or physical welfare. I thank God that at last I have been led to see the error of my ways, and that there is still time for me to undo in some measure what I have done, and to make amends for the past in the present and future. Now, what concerns you in this confession, firstly, is this: As senior member and three-fourths owner in the firm of Denton, Day & Co., I am about to assume the responsibility of its business, and to introduce new methods in its various systems which I have every reason to believe will not meet with your approval. To be absolutely fair and square, I will tell you what a few of these changes will be. I cannot tell them all, because that would be impossible. They will develop day by day as the necessity arises and confronts me. If it is possible I shall run this store in future on a Christian basis, or, in other words, on the basis of physical and moral justice, and whether the experiment proves disastrous or successful, I shall follow it to the end. I shall sink or swim as the Lord permits me."

As he finished, he looked calmly at the faces of his two partners. There was no excitement visible in his manner, except that he breathed a little heavier. For a moment only blank consternation reigned, then Mr. Day drew himself up with a scornful air, while Mr. Forbes sat staring at him with his head bowed upon his bosom.

"And suppose we do not give our consent to these changes that you speak of?" said Mr. Day, curtly. "Do you forget, Mr. Denton, that this partnership has still several years to run? Whether we own much or little of the capital, we are still your partners!"

"And as such you are at liberty to oppose my actions," answered Mr. Denton, quickly; "but in that case I shall resort to the most extreme measures, for my mind is made up, and my decision final!"

CHAPTER XXV
MR. DENTON GIVES SOME ORDERS

At this demonstration of firmness on Mr. Denton's part, Mr. Forbes still sat speechless with his head bowed sullenly. Mr. Day, on the contrary, nearly exploded with wrath, but at each angry suggestion he was met with the same firm refusal.

"Are we to be made laughing stocks for the whole business world to jeer at?" he asked as he paced the office furiously, "or to be bankrupted through methods that border strongly on insanity? For it is nothing else, Mr. Denton, but raving lunacy! No man in his sober senses would entertain such a plan for the space of a second! Why, your orders about those sweat-shops were simply ridiculous! Are we to pay more for our goods than they are really worth, and then make a charity organization of ourselves and give them to our customers?"

Mr. Denton smiled sadly. He was not at all surprised.

What amused him most was the demeanor of Mr. Forbes; he had expected vituperations from him at every point of his confession.

"You are free to rid yourself of all association with the firm," was Mr. Denton's only answer. "I will buy you out at your own figure, Mr. Day; or, as I said before, I will end the thing at once. I will apply at once to have a receiver appointed."

"But I don't wish to be bought out, and I don't wish to dissolve partnership. This store is making a fortune for us all. I would be a fool to throw over such a magnificent investment!"

> "It profiteth nothing, and fearful the cost,
>
> To gain the whole world if thy soul shall be lost!"

Mr. Denton quoted the words soberly, almost reverently. As he did so a vision of Faith Marvin rose suddenly before him.

"Pshaw! You have lost your senses, Denton!" cried Mr. Day. "Am I to be scared into idiocy by the words of some fanatic?"

"You have said nothing, Mr. Forbes," said Mr. Denton, turning from Mr. Day quietly.

"I have nothing to say," remarked Mr. Forbes, gruffly. "It is as Mr. Day says; you have lost your senses."

Mr. Denton sighed heavily. He was a little disappointed.

"You can talk the matter over by yourselves," he said, finally, "and remember, I stand ready to deal fairly by my partners. My loss, if I have one, need not be theirs; you have only to state a willingness to comply or settle."

He walked out of the office, closing the door behind him. A second later he had arrived at the door of his own office.

"Please, sir, may I see you a minute, sir?" asked a voice just behind him.

He turned and recognized Sam Watkins, the boy who had stolen the five hundred dollars.

"Come in, Sam," he said, kindly. The child looked at him in surprise. The moment the door closed behind him he burst out crying.

"Come, come, boy, don't cry! I won't scold you," said Mr. Denton, smiling.

He took Sam's hand in his own and patted it encouragingly.

"I couldn't help it, sir; indeed, I couldn't!" he blurted out. "Poor ma was so sick and needed money so dreadful!"

"So you took it for your mother," said Mr. Denton. "Now, tell me the truth, Sam; what did you do with the other three hundred dollars?"

Sam Watkins looked up into the gentleman's face. His eyes were red from weeping, but they did not waver.

"I lost it, sir," he said, simply. "It was in my coat pocket. You see, I divided the wad, sir, so it wouldn't look so bulky!"

"And did your mother scold you?" asked Mr. Denton, still smiling.

The boy's glance fell to the floor and he shifted his feet uneasily.

"No, sir, she didn't scold—that is, not exactly," he said, sniffing. "She just talked to me, sir, and then she cried something awful!"

Mr. Denton turned his head away for about a minute. There was something in the boy's story that affected him strangely. The poor woman had wept because her boy had stolen some money, yet rich men smiled complacently over what they called "good bargains," but which in reality were little more than thieving.

"How is your brother?" he asked, when he could trust himself to speak.

The boy's lips trembled and he began crying before he answered.

"He's pretty bad, sir; in the hospital," he whispered, brokenly. "They think he'll die! You see, his sweetheart, Miss Jennings, died the very day after I stole the money, and the two things, with his hard work, knocked poor Fred out completely."

"Was Miss Jennings his sweetheart?" asked Mr. Denton in astonishment. This was a phase of that horror that he had not even dreamed of.

"Oh, yes, they were sweethearts," said the boy, with a hysterical giggle. "They was awfully in love, but they couldn't afford to get married."

Mr. Denton rose from his desk and paced the office floor. The misery in the situation was even blacker than he had realized.

"See here, boy!" he said suddenly. "Give me your mother's address, and here's a ten-dollar bill for her. Now, go home and take care of her."

The boy's face flushed crimson as he refused the money.

"I wouldn't dare to take it," he muttered sheepishly. "She'd think I stole it."

"Then I'll send it by mail," said Mr. Denton quickly, "and I'll tell her at the same time that we don't mind about the three hundred. We can forgive a boy who only stole to help a sick mother."

"Oh, sir!" cried the boy. But he could get no farther. The next second he was shaking with a storm of sobs. The agony of his repentance had reached its limit. Before he left the building the letter had been posted to his mother through the pneumatic mailing tube that opened in Mr. Denton's office.

Mr. Denton's next duty was to see his buyers. He was still smarting with indignation over that "sweatshop" horror.

In less than an hour he had them all assembled in the receiving-room, which was piled from end to end with the products of underpaid labor.

His speech to them was short but decidedly to the point. They were to submit the names of the persons or firms whom they bought of, and receive his express commands concerning all further orders.

"I cannot have the souls of these poor creatures on my conscience any longer," he said at the conclusion of his statements. "So, if the public still want these goods, we will make them ourselves and pay those poor seamstresses what they are worth, besides letting them work in cleanly surroundings."

"But, Mr. Denton," spoke up one of the buyers who was a privileged character in the establishment, "that will entail endless work for the cashier's department, as well as work-rooms. As it is now, there is but one bill to pay where by your plan there would be a hundred or more, and, besides, we have no work-rooms to spare; we are already overcrowded."

"I know it," replied Mr. Denton, sadly, "and as I am well aware that reformation, like charity, should 'begin at home,' I must wait a little before putting my plan into action."

"My girls will never work with those people, I am sure," remarked the foreman of the work-rooms. "You have no idea what sticklers they are for caste. Why, as poor as they are, they turn up their noses at those beneath them!"

Mr. Denton smiled grimly at this information.

"They share that failing with the whole human family," he said, slowly. "Only a few are exempt from this feeling of scorn; they are the few who have learned to love their fellow-beings, however," he went on more cheerfully, "we who have set them this example of thoughtlessness and neglect must try to undo what we have done by patient precept and example."

His hearers stared at him, but they were too polite to reply. It was their opinion that the man had suddenly became deranged. They did not doubt for a moment that they would go on as usual.

After a few more arguments as to the impracticability of his suggestions, the men dispersed, casting meaning glances at each other.

Once beyond his hearing, they talked the startling situation over. Not one of them had ever heard of a similar occurrence.

Mr. Denton went back to his office to think a little. When he reached it he found Mr. Day pacing the floor as he waited for him.

"So your decision is final," he bellowed, as Mr. Denton entered. "You have fully decided to make a fool of yourself and wreck the firm, and all because you have not head enough to keep your religion out of business!"

Mr. Denton's face flushed, but he spoke as calmly as ever.

"If religion is needed anywhere, it is needed in business," he said quietly. "If I am a fool at all it is because I did not find it out sooner."

"Very well, then," roared Mr. Day. "I refuse to submit to such nonsense! Furthermore, as Mr. Forbes will not hear of dissolution, I shall expect you and him to buy me out at once! I will sell my right, title and interest for one hundred thousand dollars."

"But that is four times what you put in," said Mr. Denton, quickly, "and as you have already been paid a large interest on your investment, your price is exorbitant; are you too angry to see it?"

"I should have gotten that out of it before the expiration of the partnership. It is that figure or nothing," said Mr. Day, doggedly, "and, mind, I will fight against dissolution, tooth and nail, Mr. Denton. I would be as mad as you are if I did not do so!"

"Then I will pay you that amount at once, Mr. Day," said the gentleman. "I will give you a check on my personal bank account and acquire your interest as a private investment. Your price is too exorbitant to permit my purchasing it for the firm, but we will attend to the details when Mr. Forbes is present."

CHAPTER XXVI
SOME STARTLING CHANGES

As the days went by the employees of the big department store became gradually aware that something had happened. The first intimation came from the daily papers, in which was given a more or less truthful account of Mr. Day's withdrawal from the firm on the grounds that he disapproved of his senior partner's new business methods.

What these methods were it remained to be seen. The clerks were hopeful of some reforms, but for a while they only wondered and waited.

Miss Fairbanks stopped at Faith's counter early one morning, when the store was comparatively empty, and began talking to her in an unusually affable manner.

"There's something going to happen here soon," she said, confidently. "And, in my opinion, it's going to be pretty serious. Either Mr. Denton has got religion, or else he's gone crazy, for he's giving us buyers a lot of orders nowadays that will mean the failure of the firm if we are obliged to obey them."

"Why, what are they, Miss Fairbanks?" Faith asked in surprise. Miss Jones came up also and listened for the answer.

"Well, in the first place, we are not to beat down the drummers any more, but are to offer them fair prices on all our orders. Then we are to learn, if possible, who makes the goods that we buy, for Mr. Denton says he does not want to make a profit out of some poor woman's work while she is going half clothed and perhaps sick and starving."

"Why, the man is stark mad," said Miss Jones, in amazement. "As if it was any concern of his what other people work for!"

"I think he is quite right," remarked Faith, very soberly. "I can understand how he feels, and I think he is very brave to give such orders."

"Then he says," went on Miss Fairbanks, "that there are to be new arrangements for you girls. You are to be relieved every two hours for about twenty minutes. That means, of course, that he is going to hire a lot of new help, and I, for one, am sorry, for there'll be blunders by the hundred."

"Oh, perhaps not," said Faith, brightly. "I hope not, anyway, for your sake, Miss Fairbanks. I know just how annoying it is for you, who have so many clerks to look after."

Miss Fairbanks looked at her gratefully, but with a little surprise. It was not often that one of her girls expressed any sympathy for her.

"Then, there's to be a full hour at luncheon," continued the buyer after a minute, "and the best of all is that we are to have a new lunch-room. No more eating in that rat hole down in the basement."

"Well, that is good news," said Miss Jones delightedly. "Really, I begin to think that the millennium is coming!"

"Or the Kingdom of God," said Faith, very happily. "There is no doubt in my mind but that Mr. Denton has become a Christian."

Both women stared at her as she spoke, but, for a wonder, neither of them scoffed at her statement.

Miss Fairbanks recovered herself first and asked a very natural question.

"What do you mean by saying that he has become a Christian? Why, Mr. Denton has been a member of the church ever since I can remember."

"Alas!" sighed Faith sadly. "That doesn't always signify, Miss Fairbanks. He may have accepted Christ but not Christ's spirit; but it is plain now that the very essence of godliness is awakening within him. If this is so I can predict that there will be great changes in this store and that every one will be for the comfort of its toilers."

A few customers coming in cut short the conversation, and as Maggie Brady was absent the department was short-handed, as usual, so that there was only an odd minute or two for idling.

"I wonder if Miss Brady is ill?" said Faith as she squeezed by Miss Jones in the narrow space behind the counter.

"It will go hard with her if she doesn't show up pretty soon," was the answer, "for between you and me, I believe Gunning hates her."

"Oh, these dreadful hatreds," said Faith, with a sigh. "Poor Miss Brady looks so wretched. I don't see how any one can hate her."

"Well, you see, she was engaged to Gunning once, and she might better have married him than to have thrown herself away on Jim Denton."

Cash girl Number 83 came up as she spoke. She was the girl who had first told Faith that Mr. Watkins was very ill and in the hospital, and it was evident by her manner that she had something else to tell her.

"What is it, 83?" asked Faith, expectantly. "Have you heard any news of Mr. Watkins' condition?"

"Yes, and I've heard more'n that," said the little girl quickly, "but I won't spring it all on you at once, for it might shock you, Miss Marvin."

Faith was puzzled at her words, but she tried to restrain her eagerness until the girl had given a package to a customer and come back to the counter.

"Mr. Watkins is better—lots better," she said, gayly. "They say the boss has been to see him in his howling swell carriage, and they've fixed up the matter about the money all right; they must have, because Sammy Watkins is back in his old position."

"Oh, that is lovely," cried Faith, clasping her hands together.

"Well, the rest ain't so lovely!" said the cash girl, grinning, "for I saw Mag Brady on the street last night. She was drunk as a toper, and she says she's a-goin' to 'do' you!"

"What!" gasped Faith, in astonishment as the cash girl finished, "Miss Brady intoxicated! You surely don't mean it?"

"Oh, don't I?" said the child, with a worldly leer. "I mean lots more than that, only I'm too nice to say it."

She walked away to answer another call while Faith stared first at Miss Fairbanks and then at Miss Jones. Both had heard the words yet they were laughing at her amazement.

"You are easily shocked," said Miss Fairbanks, with a shrug. "Why, any one with half an eye could see that Mag Brady loves whiskey."

"That's another thing that Jim Denton taught her," said Miss Jones indifferently. "Why, I knew Mag Brady when she was as innocent as you are."

"But can nothing be done to reclaim her?" asked Faith, eagerly. "You say you knew her when she was different, Miss Jones; have you ever tried to save her from ruin?"

"I mind my own business," said Miss Jones, haughtily, "and I find that is all I can possibly do. Mag Brady must save herself if she wants to be saved, but, between you and me, I don't think she wants to."

"But you—you are her friend," Faith cried, turning to Miss Fairbanks; "do promise me that you will plead with her; it might do wonders! Just think how you would feel if the poor girl was your sister!"

Miss Fairbanks seemed earnest and sincere as she replied:

"I will certainly advise her if she gives me the chance. Poor girl, I am sorry for her, but I doubt if I can save her."

"Then we must all pray that God will do so," whispered Faith, very soberly. "It is a wrong that we will all be held responsible for; to see her going down to destruction and not try to save her!"

Miss Jones wheeled around and went to a customer, but Miss Fairbanks paused and looked at Faith for a moment.

"I would give the world to possess your faith," she said, hesitatingly; "but there's no use—no use—I'm too great a sinner."

There was no chance to reply, for she walked away as she spoke. In a second she was talking to a customer in her usual business-like manner. As Faith turned to look over her stock she heard some one speak.

There was a colored man at her counter holding a letter out toward her.

"Dis yere lettah fo' you, missy," he said, with a wide grin. "Dar ain't no name on it, honey, but I know's yo' face. Yo' is num'er fo' eleben. Reckin ain't no 'stake 'bout it!"

"I am Number 411, certainly," said Faith, politely, "but I can't imagine who would write me a letter; still, if you are sure it's for me, I suppose I must accept."

"Oh, it's fo' you all right," said the negro, decidedly, "fo' de capting p'inted yo' out on de street las' ebenin'."

Faith took the letter and opened it hastily. As she glanced rapidly over the writing she blushed as red as a poppy.

"Got a mash note?" asked Miss Jones with a careless glance at the letter.

"Not exactly," stammered Faith, "but it is almost as unpleasant. It is from a man whom Bob Hardy spoke to me about—a fellow who thinks because I am poor that he can buy my soul with his superfluous money!"

CHAPTER XXVII
THE POISONED CANDY

But Faith had only read a part of the letter when she made her statement, for, on a closer perusal, she found she was mistaken. If the writer had ever dreamed of tempting her with the lure of proffered luxury he admitted his change of opinion in terms of honest candor.

"Dear Child," the letter read, "since our meeting the other evening I have been thinking constantly how I best could win your esteem and affection. That I should desire the friendship of a pure, young girl would sound strange to the ears of many worldly people, but to you, who are as distant from worldliness as are the angels in heaven, the suggestion can bring only bewildering sensations. To say that I am ashamed does not half express my feelings. To say that I wish to make immediate amends does not convey to you the half of my eagerness in that direction.

"Will you allow me to call upon you at your home? This is the request of a man who was once a gentleman, but who, through the bitterness of disappointment, had lost faith in all things holy."

The letter was signed "Cornelius C. Deering."

Faith read it over and over—the signature was in a measure familiar, but just at that time she could not place it.

As she tucked the letter in her pocket, Mr. Gunning approached the counter. He was twirling his mustache with his coarse, blunt fingers, and there was a superciliousness in his manner that was almost disgusting.

"Perhaps you are not aware, Number 411, that we don't allow that sort of thing here," he said in a loud tone. "If you must have such improper notes from men, please see that they are not delivered during business hours. I can't have you wasting time in reading letters!"

For a moment the floor seemed sinking beneath Faith's feet, but it was not altogether from the effect of his words—it was the shock of finding out that Miss Jones was treacherous.

For a moment it seemed incomprehensible that she should have repeated her remark, but how else could the floor-walker have guessed that her letter was either from a "man" or "improper"?

She almost bit her tongue in her effort to keep silent, and at first she was even tempted to show the fellow the letter.

"It was not my fault that the letter came to me here," she said finally. "Believe me, Mr. Gunning, it would not have happened if I could have prevented it."

"Oh, of course, you can't help men writing love letters to you," said the fellow, impudently; "but if I see any more of them I shall report it to Mr. Gibson! Our rules are very strict. There is to be no flirting in the building!"

Faith would have liked to ask him why he did not stop James Denton from flirting in the store, and why the detectives were not punished for their villainous efforts in behalf of outsiders, as well as a dozen more questions, some of which would have included his own department, but she was far too wise to risk such a venture.

When Mr. Gunning walked away, Miss Jones came up to her. There was a sneer on her face while her eyes twinkled with amusement.

"How could you be so mean as to tell him?" Faith asked, breathlessly. "You saw how distressed I was; why could you not respect my feelings?"

"Oh, I guess you didn't feel so bad as you try to make out," said Miss Jones, snappishly. "Girls that make friends with men who keep nigger servants ain't always as green as they look, you know! Sometimes they are worse than those who ain't so smooth or so clever!"

"You are as insulting as he was," said Faith, very gravely. "I am disappointed in you, Miss Jones. I though you were more friendly."

"Well, who cares what you thought?" was the heartless answer. "I'm not to blame if you took me for a fool! Why, even Mag Brady could see through your sly actions!"

Faith looked at her in astonishment, her veins throbbing with indignation.

"She understood your little game that day of the fire, when you and Jim Denton were talking together! He's rich, Jim Denton is, and he's mighty susceptible! You ain't such an innocent but what you found that out, and now he is meeting you on street corners and sending you candy!"

Faith had heard all she could bear, so she turned and walked slowly away. She was so confused that for an hour or more she could hardly make out her checks properly.

The new packer was a girl about two years her junior, and as Faith handed up her goods she could not help thinking of Miss Jennings.

Poor Mary, with all her bitterness, had been a true, loyal friend. She would have scorned to do a treacherous or dishonest action herself, yet she absolutely refused to condemn such conduct in others.

Faith remembered her plea for the thief, Lou Willis, and that led her finally on a new train of thought, so that she was able to almost forget her late conversation.

Several times during the day there were changes made in the department, and Miss Fairbanks was kept busy altering the prices on goods, especially on what were known as the "bargain counters."

These counters were principally small tables standing here and there in the aisles, and during the rush hours they were always surrounded by customers.

Finally, to the surprise of the entire department, the tables, themselves, were removed, Mr. Denton coming down from his office to superintend the transaction.

"The fire company has warned him again, I guess," whispered Miss Fairbanks to Faith. "Well, that's a hard one on Mag Brady; she was hired expressly for those bargains."

"He will surely make a place for her elsewhere, will he not?" asked Faith. "It would be dreadful if the poor girl should lose her work completely!"

"She deserves it," said Cash Number 83, who was standing near. "'Tain't as if she was stayin' away 'cause she was sick! She's just on a spree along with some girls and fellers!"

"What gets me is how Mr. Forbes is taking all these changes. He don't seem to be saying a word," continued Miss Fairbanks, without noticing the cash girl.

"Oh, he's just saying nothing and sawing wood," said Miss Jones, knowingly. "He's too foxy to quit the firm as old Pomposity did! Probably he thinks it won't last, and he's willing to wait till it's over."

"Well, it will be a great deal safer here now without the tables," said the buyer. "If we have a fire now there won't be so much crowding."

"They say he's doing this sort of thing all over the store," said Mr. Gunning, who had just returned from helping with the tables.

"Then they tell me, too, that he's having a lunch-room and restaurant for employees built on the sixth floor of the building. All the goods that were stored there are being taken to the basement."

"And we cash girls are all to be fired!" spoke up "Number 83," sadly, "except those who are healthy and over fourteen. The rest of us that ain't got any parents have got to go to Gerry's, or, if we have got parents, they've got to support us—that's what the boss says, but it sounds mighty like a 'pipe dream.'"

"It sounds like a sensible arrangement," said Faith, seriously, "for it's a shame that such children should have to work! Why, you ought to be in school this very minute!"

"Well, I'd rather be here," said "83" very shortly. "There ain't no fun in a school-room, and what's the good of studyin', anyhow?"

"But don't you wish to be able to cipher and to read books?" said Faith.

"What's the use?" was the answer; "they don't tell you nothin', at least not nothin' about how to earn your livin'!"

Faith gave up in despair. She was baffled at every turn. The only ray of sunshine that she could see was in Mr. Denton's rapidly developing improvements.

As she mounted the stairs to the sixth floor to eat her luncheon in the new quarters, she was surprised to find Sam Watkins waiting at the top of the last flight, apparently on the lookout for her.

"This is Miss Marvin, ain't it?" he asked when he saw her, at the same time drawing a package out from under his jacket. "I was told to give you this," he whispered, shyly. "Here, take it, quick, while there ain't no one lookin'! Them gals would turn green if they knowed you had a whole box of candy!"

Faith took the box and looked at it sharply. There was no card this time, but she felt sure it was from James Denton.

"You can have it, Sam," she said, without an instant's hesitation. "I really don't care for it; do take it, Sam. But, by the way, where did you get it?"

"Hush!"

The boy whispered the word with his fingers on his lips.

"There they come now, miss! Are you sure you don't want it?"

"Quite sure, Sam," was Faith's answer, as she hurried away. She did not wish the clerks to know that she had been the recipient of more presents.

Sam Watkins took the box directly to the men's lunch-room, which was on the same floor at the other end of the building.

Being a boy, he could not long resist the temptation of candy, but just as he opened the box with a grimace of delight, Ben Tyler came in carrying a wide-awake, little Skye terrier.

"I just found him in the store; some lady has lost him, I guess," said Tyler, as the others all looked at him. "I was going to send him to the 'Found desk,' but he wouldn't have it. He sticks to me as if I was his master."

"I'll get him away from you, I'll bet!" said Sam, holding out a piece of candy.

In a second the dog sprang out of Tyler's arms and swallowed the sweetmeat greedily.

"There, you can't have any more," said Sam, after he had fed him a couple more pieces. "I've got to treat the rest of the crowd, and there won't be enough to go around."

"Keep your candy, kid; we don't want it," said one of the men good-naturedly, but Sam was so interested in watching the lively little dog that, fortunately, he forgot to eat for a few minutes.

"Hello! What ails the dog?" exclaimed Tyler, suddenly. "How queer he acts! I believe the stuff has made him sick already!"

All eyes were turned on the poor little creature, and it was soon plain to be seen that he was suffering terribly.

"It ought not to hurt him," said one of the men.

"Not if it's all right," said Tyler, going over toward Sam. "Let me see your candy, my boy; I believe there's something wrong with it."

Sam dropped the chocolate that he was just conveying to his mouth, and handed the box to the detective with great alacrity.

"There's something in it, I'm sure," he said, after a careful scrutiny, "and I'm willing to bet the stuff is poisoned!"

A final moan from the poor little dog fully justified him in his decision.

"The dog is dead," said one of the clerks in a solemn voice. "So there isn't a shadow of doubt but what the candy is poisoned."

CHAPTER XXVIII
A PAINFUL SITUATION

To say that Sam was disappointed would be describing his feelings very mildly, but in an instant the discomfiture was forgotten in a new sensation—he had suddenly thought of Miss Marvin's good fortune.

Suppose she had kept the box and eaten the candy! The thought frightened Sam out of all further idea of secrecy.

In an instant he had related how he came by the candy, and the clerks were looking at each other with questioning glances.

"'Tain't the first box of candy she's had sent her," said one. "I heard Fairbanks say that she got them often from Jim Denton."

"Yes, she's cut Mag Brady out for good in that direction. Well, why shouldn't she? She's new and as pretty as a picture!"

"But, surely, Jim Denton didn't send this box," said the detective. "If he's sweet on the girl he wouldn't want to poison her."

"Well, hardly, Tyler," laughed another of the lunchers.

"Perhaps he intended it for Mag," suggested another. "If he's tired of the girl he may be trying to fix her."

"Pshaw! He doesn't have to resort to such measures as that! What could a poor girl do to injure Jim Denton? No, Tyler, you'll have to look somewhere else for your poisoner, I reckon," said one of the oldest men in the whole establishment.

"Who gave you the box in the first place?" asked the detective of Sam. "I mean, who told you to give it to Miss Marvin?"

Sam spoke up promptly, for he had nothing to hide.

"A kid gave it to me at the door—a messenger boy—who said he was in a tearing hurry."

"Did you sign for it?" asked the detective, looking sharply at the boy.

"Naw, I didn't sign nothin'; he didn't have no ticket."

"Then he wasn't a messenger at all," was the reply, "and you are a big dunce, Sam Watkins, that you didn't know it!"

"Well, I thought it was straight, anyhow," whispered the boy. "How was I to guess that some one was tryin' to pisen Miss Marvin?"

Ben Tyler took the box carefully and replaced the wrapper; then, telling Sam to follow, he went straight to Mr. Denton's office.

"Now, Sam, tell Mr. Denton exactly what you have told me," said the detective, after he had stated what had happened.

Sam repeated his story without the slightest variation. Mr. Denton cross-questioned him, but there was nothing further to learn. A boy had handed the box to Sam and told him to give it to Miss Faith Marvin.

After Mr. Denton and the detective had examined the candy carefully they held a consultation as to what should be done about it.

"We must have it analyzed at once," said Mr. Denton, anxiously. "That is the only way of proving the matter."

The detective nodded. He knew that came first, but it needed no analysis to convince him that the candy was poisoned.

"Has she ever received a similar box that you know of?" asked Mr. Denton.

The detective hesitated for a moment. He hardly knew how to tell him.

"I believe she has, sir," he said, after a minute; "but I would advise you to ask the young woman herself, for I can only repeat what may be idle gossip."

"You are right," said Mr. Denton, touching an electric button and sending the boy who answered to the department for Miss Marvin.

In less than five minutes Faith entered the office, but before he came the detective slipped a newspaper over the box of poisoned candy, and a nod of the head showed that Mr. Denton understood and approved of the movement.

"Miss Marvin," said Mr. Denton, "I wish you to answer a question: Are you in the habit of receiving boxes of candy as presents?"

With Mr. Gunning's remarks still burning in her brain, Faith could not help blushing at this unexpected question.

She finally controlled herself and answered firmly:

"I have never received but two boxes since I entered your employ, sir—one a few days ago and the other this morning."

"What did you do with the candy?" asked her employer again.

"I gave the first box to a cash girl who works in my department, and the other I gave to Sam. I didn't even open them."

"Why did you not open them?" asked the detective, sharply.

Faith glanced at Mr. Denton a moment before replying.

"Yes, why did you not open them? Are you not fond of candy, Miss Marvin?"

"I like it, yes, sir," was Faith's slow answer; "but the gift was unexpected. In fact, sir, I did not want it, and so I gave away the candy because I objected to the giver."

Faith's color had risen as she said these words, and she seemed to brace herself mentally for what was coming.

Should she answer the next question, which she felt sure would follow? It was a moment that taxed all the decision in her nature.

Mr. Denton looked at her smilingly as he prepared for the question. There was not an inkling in his brain of the true situation.

"Do you object, Miss Marvin, to telling us who sent it? Really, the question is important, or I would not ask it."

Faith looked from one to the other and clenched her fingers convulsively. It seemed cruel to her to thus wound the feelings of another.

"I would rather not tell, please, Mr. Denton," she began.

"Then I must insist," said the gentleman, "for, as I said, the matter is serious."

"If you insist, I must obey," said Faith, in some bewilderment; "but I beg you will forgive me for saying that your son sent me the candy."

Before the words were fairly out Mr. Denton was pale with horror. The shock was so great that he shuddered as he looked at her.

"My son," he whispered, hoarsely. "Is that true, Miss Marvin? Is my son one of the rascals who annoy the young women under my protection? Is he—"

He could get no farther—his feelings overcame him.

"I am afraid he is," said Faith, very faintly, "for I have given him no right to be sending me presents."

Mr. Denton leaned back in his chair with one hand to his brow. The detective's ruse in covering the candy had produced results as startling as they were suspicious.

If Faith had known of the poison in the candy no power could have induced her to tell what she had, but up to the present she was in total ignorance of the matter, and it was now Mr. Denton's turn to dread the next disclosures.

"My dear child," he said at last; "I have something to tell you—something that will shock you even more than your news shocks me; it is this, your box of candy to-day was poisoned."

Faith stared at him stupidly for the space of a second, then the full situation dawned slowly upon her. "If that is the case, your son did not send it, Mr. Denton!" she cried in decided accents, "for although he is thoughtless and careless of others, he would shrink from doing such a deed as that, even though he had a motive, which he certainly hasn't!"

"I believe you," said Mr. Denton, in a tone of relief. "Whoever sent the candy is making my son the scapegoat! You say there was no writing on the package when you got it, young man, and no message or card when you opened it in the lunch-room?"

"I can vouch for that," said Tyler, as the boy shook his head. "I was watching the boy when he opened the candy."

"Have you any enemies in the store that you know of, Miss Marvin—any one who is aware that my son has sent you candy?"

Mr. Denton had turned toward Faith as he asked the question.

"More enemies than friends, I am afraid, sir," was the answer, "for although I have tried my best to be friendly with the girls, they all treat me coldly; they are not at all like Miss Jennings."

"It is strange how they dislike and distrust each other," said Mr. Denton, sadly. "But I suppose it is because they have so little in life, they are constantly filled with envy over the possessions of others."

If Faith knew this to be a compliment she did not show it. So far it had not seemed to her that the girls were envious of her beauty.

"You may go now, Sam," said Mr. Denton, kindly, "and, see here, young man, keep your mouth shut about this matter! Not a single word until I give you permission!"

Sam promised faithfully, and was glad to do so. Since he had been restored to his position he had silently worshiped Mr. Denton.

"Now, Miss Marvin, I must caution you as I did Sam," said the gentleman. "Say nothing until the officer here has ferreted out this matter. A single word might put the criminal on guard, and a single utterance may delay the triumph of justice."

He dismissed the young girl with a courteous bow, and was surprised that she still lingered in a pleading manner.

"Please, Mr. Denton," she cried, brokenly, "don't try to ferret the matter out! I beg of you, sir, let it drop and keep it a secret! The injury to your son is no greater than to me, so let it go no further, I implore it, Mr. Denton!"

"What, pass an attempted murder by!" exclaimed Mr. Denton in amazement. "I am astonished, Miss Marvin, that you should make such a suggestion!"

"But I do make it!" cried Faith desperately, "and I beg that you will grant it! Surely it was I who was to be the victim. I should be allowed to forgive the culprit!"

"On what grounds?" asked Mr. Denton, who was trying to exercise justice.

"On the grounds that it will do no good to expose or punish," cried Faith eagerly, "for a person who could do a deed like that can be saved by mercy, but not by justice!"

Mr. Denton looked thoughtfully, but he could not accede to her request. He did not believe that even a Christian could ignore the laws of man in such a matter.

"No, Miss Marvin," he said, firmly, "the criminal must be exposed. It is the only way to stop a repetition of such cowardly actions!"

"It was a woman who did it without doubt!" broke in the detective sharply, "and she'll do it again, sure, if she isn't punished! A woman that hates like that will stop at nothing!"

Faith glanced at him reproachfully, but did not answer. She did not mean by word or look to betray her suspicions.

"I will not ask you to state whom you suspect, Miss Marvin," said Mr. Denton, "for I see in your face that you would not tell me; but in regard to my son, I must talk with you later. You are under my protection, and not even my own flesh and blood shall be allowed to annoy you."

"I am sure it is not his wish to annoy me," said Faith. "He just doesn't understand that some girls are different from others. He has met only the weak ones who could not withstand his flattery, but I can take care of myself, sir, or, if not, God will protect me."

"Alas! you do not know human nature yet, my child," said Mr. Denton, gazing at her with an expression of almost fatherly interest, "but pray always that your trust may be as steadfast as now—that it will never be shattered on the rocks of sorrow and misfortune."

Faith passed out of his presence with a last pleading glance—she seemed to be mutely imploring his mercy toward the guilty.

CHAPTER XXIX
A VISITOR AT THE FLAT

For the next few days Faith heard no more about the box of poisoned candy, but she was not allowed to entirely forget it, for Ben Tyler, the detective, almost haunted the department.

If he was looking for the culprit there he did not show it, for he laughed and chatted with all the girls whenever he had an opportunity.

Maggie Brady had come back to find her "bargain counter" gone, but Miss Fairbanks had already received orders to put her behind the regular counter.

This brought Faith and Maggie nearer together than ever, and the hatred in Maggie's face was very apparent, although she schooled herself to be fairly pleasant.

Faith treated her as kindly as possible, but for all that she occasionally caught Maggie glaring at her between half closed lids in a manner that thrilled her with fresh suspicions.

At those times Faith felt a nervousness that she could not control. She almost dreaded to turn her back upon the morbid young woman.

More than once she thought of Lou Willis' words that "Maggie Brady was a sneak and a coward, who waited until dark before attacking the object of her hatred."

But this always led her to think of Lou Willis, herself, and to question over and over her well meant decision to try and help the girl to be honest by not reporting her dishonesty.

She met Lou often now, and always talked to her cordially, but she could feel that she made slow headway into the young woman's confidence.

"You and I are so different," Miss Willis said one day. "You seem to enjoy playing the proprieties, while I just hate them!"

"But I don't think I am altogether proper, as you call it," Faith answered. "I do lots of things that are not conventional and lots that are unusual, still I always try to follow my conscience."

"Conscience, what's that?" asked Lou, with a grimace. "They made me without one I guess, and I'm mighty glad of it!"

"But surely you wish to do right, don't you, Miss Willis?"

Faith's eyes were eager with hope as she asked the question.

"Oh, what difference does it make whether I do or don't? Do what you please and don't get caught, that's my motto!" laughed the girl.

"But you surely will get caught some day," said Faith soberly. "No one can ignore or break the laws of God and man without being ultimately brought to punishment or repentance."

"Well, so far as the laws of God go, I'm not worrying," said Lou, with a shrug. "He made me as I am and as He wanted me, I suppose. I'm sure I hope He's satisfied with His creation! If He ain't, He can make me over if He's so almighty powerful, but when it comes to the laws of man, why that's a different matter."

"And how do you regard those?" asked Faith, trying hard not to be shocked. The woman's answer came like a clap of thunder.

"I look upon man's laws as my natural enemies," she said sullenly. "They are made by a lot of people who know nothing of misery or starvation, and who are as incompetent to judge my actions as I am to judge theirs. In other words, man's laws are all institutions of the devil! They force you to steal and then punish you for doing so!"

After a little of this reasoning Faith grew more helpless than ever. It was like trying to melt an iceberg with a sunbeam to thaw that callous nature. Only Lou's violent temper and intense hatred of her enemies kept the woman from being adamant in matters moral or spiritual.

She surprised Faith frequently with her outbursts of remorse, the most of which were bestowed in the direction of Miss Brady.

"I saw her smiling at you to-day," she said to Faith one night. "Look out for her, Miss Innocent, that's when she's most likely to stab you!"

Faith trembled for fear that Lou would hear in some way of the box of poisoned candy, but strangely enough it had been hushed up for the present.

Some power, unknown to Faith, had stopped every tongue from blabbing.

"I expect it is some of Mr. Denton's good work," she said to her mother one night as they sat at supper with little Dick between them. "If he can stop the gossip in the store he will accomplish a great deal, for I believe half of the bad friendships between the clerks are made through idle gossip."

"He is doing wonders," sighed Mrs. Marvin in answer. "At last I am hearing of what looks to be conscientious Christianity."

"You will hear of much more, I am sure, mother," said Faith, "for I am told that Mr. Forbes intends to remain in the firm, and that looks as if he indorsed Mr. Denton."

"Or awaiting the outcome," added her mother quietly. She could never quite accept her daughter's innocent reasoning.

While they were still talking, a letter was delivered from Mr. Watkins.

He was "doing nicely at the hospital," he said, and "on the straight road to recovery," but what was better still, Mr. Denton was coming for his mother and had assured him that his position at the store was still open to him.

"Mr. Forbes must certainly acquiesce to that, mother," said Faith again, "for Mr. Watkins was his office assistant; Mr. Denton would hardly put him back if his partner was not willing."

Mrs. Marvin was about to reply when their bell rang sharply. Both rose from the table and went into the little parlor. A moment later some one tapped at the door, and Faith opened it promptly. She confronted an acquaintance; it was the man whom she had met, and who had written her the note signed "Cornelius C. Deering."

For an instant Faith was shocked out of every semblance of hospitality. She stood staring at the man as if he were an intruder.

Like a flash it passed through her mind that she had not answered his letter, and that he had presumed upon that silence to force his presence upon her. The next instant she was brought swiftly back to her senses, for the man was staring back at her as though she were a ghost, and the expression on his face was almost pitiful.

"What is it, sir? What has happened?" she asked, taking a step forward.

"I think I have made a mistake," said the man, huskily. "I had no idea, I assure you, of intruding upon you."

"There are twenty families in the house, so your mistake is natural," said Faith coldly. "Pray mention the name you wish, as I can probably direct you."

"I am looking for a lady and her daughter," said the man distinctly, "the lady is my sister whom I have not seen in twenty years. She is a widow, and her name is Mrs. Adelaide Marvin."

With a gasp of horror Faith staggered back into the room just as her mother sprang forward with a joyous greeting.

"Oh, Charles, my brother!" she cried, falling on his shoulder. "How I have longed to see you, you naughty boy, every day since you ran away from us in dear old England!"

CHAPTER XXX
THE UNEXPECTED FORTUNE

The next act of Faith's was one of noble heroism. In that moment of misery she forced herself to think only of her mother, thus ignoring her own position in the matter entirely.

Without a word she walked back into the kitchen, leaving brother and sister together, and taking little Dick in her lap, tried to think the matter over as calmly as possible.

It was an embarrassing position, look at it as she would, but not so much for herself as for the man whom she now knew to be her own uncle.

As the moments passed she heard her mother's voice grow more and more pleading, and although she could not hear what was being said, she conjectured rightly that she was urging her brother to accede to something, while he as steadily refused the accession.

Finally the hall door closed and Faith heard him descending the stairs. In an instant she hurried to join her mother in the parlor.

"Oh, Faith!" cried her mother, "can you believe it, dear, it was brother Charles, alive and well, when I had given him up for dead over and over again! And, Faith, you will never have to work another day, for we are almost rich, dear brother says. He has fifty thousand dollars in trust for me from my father's estate, which has only lately been settled!"

"Oh, mother, is it possible?" cried Faith in surprise; "but why did he leave so soon? You had surely not finished talking!"

Mrs. Marvin shook her head in a very perplexed manner.

"He seems sadly changed, Faith. I don't know what ails him. I begged him to wait and see my daughter, but he refused almost angrily."

"Oh, well, never mind!" replied Faith blushing. "He will probably come back again. I would not worry about it, mother."

"But I can't understand it," said Mrs. Marvin, sighing. "It seems unnatural that Charles should not wish to see my daughter."

Faith tried to cheer her, but she was almost crying herself. Another shock like this would have brought on hysterics. It had been a dreadful trial to her to keep that strange conversation from her mother, but now she was profoundly thankful that she had been able to do so, and almost involuntarily she whispered a prayer that no word of hers might ever disturb her dear mother's confidence in her only brother.

The thought of no more work did not once enter her mind. It was with some difficulty that her mother finally got her to talk about their good fortune.

"It is not for myself that I am most thankful," said Mrs. Marvin, "but I am so glad that you can be at home once more! No more wearing out soul and body in the service of others."

Faith looked at her thoughtfully before she answered.

"How soon can we have the money?" she asked.

"Right away," said Mrs. Marvin; "it is invested in this city. I have only to be identified at the bank by my brother."

"I am very glad, mother," was Faith's smiling reply, "for now we can hire a better flat and have a woman to do the work and look after everything, but about my working, dear, please don't think of that just now—really I seem to feel a little bit sorry to think that there is no need of my working."

"You mean that you are interested in those poor girls, I suppose." said her mother. "Well, there will be other ways to help them now—you need not work among them."

"But I am sure that it is the best way to be of use to them," said Faith quickly. "If they thought I had money they would not accept me seriously. They would say, as they have said of other rich women, that my interest is a 'fad' and that I could 'afford to talk religion with my pocket full of money.'"

"You have learned their arguments quickly," said Mrs. Marvin with a smile, "but listen, Faith! There is some one in the hall! It is possible that Charles has returned for something."

Faith opened the door, nervously, but a look of relief soon crossed her face. The second caller was none other than young Mr. Denton.

"Thank goodness, I've found you!" exclaimed the young man coolly. "I've been wandering around these halls for the past half hour, either I'm awfully stupid or the bells are all wrong, for I've rung them all and nobody has answered! You should supply your friends with compasses and charts, Miss Marvin, so they won't get lost when they come to see you!"

Faith had to smile, although she was a trifle indignant. She could not imagine what had brought the young man to her apartments.

"Did you wish to see me about anything?" she asked bluntly as her thoughts flew instinctively to the poisoned candy. "If you do, please come in, and I will be glad to listen."

"I do, indeed," responded the young man. "I should not have dreamed of intruding upon you without a very good reason."

Faith was almost sure it was the candy now, although she had been assured by his father that he had been told nothing about it.

As she introduced him to her mother, she was anxious and excited, and one conjecture as to his errand followed swiftly after another. When they were seated Mr. Denton started at once on his errand, and as he talked he gazed at Faith earnestly, as though trying to read her emotion.

"My errand is a purely personal one," he began, "and you ladies may think it a selfish one also, but the fact is I have come for a little assistance. I want you, Miss Marvin, to help me reason with my father."

Faith made an exclamation of unfeigned surprise.

"I don't understand," she said slowly. "What is wrong with your father, Mr. Denton?"

"That's what I'd like to know," was the emphatic answer, "but between you and I, it's my opinion that he's crazy!"

Mrs. Marvin and Faith both stared at him curiously, for this time there was more sadness than disrespect in his language.

"Listen to this," he went on quickly, "and see if I am not right! I will put the situation before you without a particle of exaggeration."

"Wait!" said Mrs. Marvin. "What does all this concern us, sir? Are you not doing wrong to talk to strangers about your father's business?"

A smile passed over the young man's features, and he turned toward Faith with a glance of admiration.

"I think not," he said shortly, "and for this simple reason—he admires your daughter above any girl that he has met; she has influenced him in the past and can influence him again in the future. And he is sadly in need of influence, I can assure you," he continued, "for, at the present moment, he is on the verge of two things, they are the verge of bankruptcy and the verge of insanity!"

Mrs. Marvin looked shocked, but Faith's brow became clearer. It was coming to her now what was troubling young Denton.

The young man went on with hardly a perceptible pause, his face growing more handsome and manly as he became interested and excited.

"My father to-day is worth a million dollars, a large percentage of it having been made in his present business. He is prominent both in social and business circles, and up to the present his ability has never been questioned. To-day he has changed all this as far as it is possible to change it in the short period of a week. He is making arrangements to transact his business on what he calls a 'religious basis,' which means that he intends to transact worldly affairs by heavenly methods, and it does not take much intelligence to see where he will terminate. He will be a bankrupt in five years, if he isn't sooner, for no fortune in the world would float such an enterprise. Now, I can't see this go on without making an effort to stop it, but as I have little or no influence with him myself, I have come to Miss Marvin to ask her to help me."

"What do you wish my daughter to do?" Mrs. Marvin asked the question with a little amusement.

"I hardly know," was his honest answer, "but if she could just induce him to think that God did not expect such a sacrifice and that it was only necessary to do good in moderation, it might act as a restraint on his wholesale generosity, put a brake, so to speak, on his downward course to failure."

"But I think it an upward course to victory!" said Faith with enthusiasm. "And you have no idea how I honor your father for taking it! Just think, Mr. Denton, what good his money can do! Why, it is a duty which he owes by right to God, for who else gave him the ability to make all this money?"

"Do you think God gave it to him?" asked Mr. Denton, quickly. "Well, I should have said that his most successful methods were invented by the devil!"

"Then it is time to put his ill-gotten wealth to good account! I am astonished, Mr. Denton, that you should wish him to retain it!"

Faith's eyes were fairly blazing now, but the look of admiration only deepened upon young Denton's features.

There was a cry from little Dick in the kitchen just then, and Mrs. Marvin rose hastily and excused herself to go to him.

"Miss Marvin," urged the young man, "don't be harsh in your judgment, please! Remember I have been used to luxury all my life. My mother has been used to it—we cannot bear to lose it."

He bent toward the young girl as he said the words, and as Faith saw the eagerness in his face, a great wave of pity surged up within her.

He was thoughtless, even wicked, but he was not altogether to blame. The very luxury that he craved was responsible for it.

"I would like to help you if I could," she said very gently, "but you surely would not have me go against my own conscience."

"No, I don't know that I would," said young Denton slowly, "for if you did you would not be what you are just now, the embodiment of all that is best and sweetest in woman."

CHAPTER XXXI
MAG BRADY'S ARREST

There was no mistaking young Denton's words or looks. Faith could not have been a woman and not understood their meaning.

For a second her lids fell in a tell-tale manner, and her cheeks paled and reddened with each alternating emotion.

She knew she must resent the young man's words at once, but her confusion of the moment rendered her powerless to do so.

Suddenly a thought of Maggie Brady flitted across her brain. It gave her strength and courage to resist the spell that was upon her.

"Your words are not sincere, I am afraid, Mr. Denton," she managed to say. "You only think to flatter me as you have numbers of others."

The young man leaned back quickly, and a flush of shame mounted to his brow.

"God forbid!" he said, sharply. "No, you wrong me, Miss Marvin! As wicked as I am, I would not insult you."

"But you did once!" said Faith, bravely. "The first day I was in the store! You bowed and smiled at me as brazenly as—as though you did not respect me!"

It was out at last, and Faith's mind was relieved. She had never quite been able to forget that occurrence.

"That was because I did not know you," explained young Denton, lamely. "I thought you might be willing to flirt a little—no one else ever refused me."

"Is it possible?"

Faith asked the question in out and out amazement. She could see by the young man's face that he was not lying.

"The other girls were always glad enough to flirt a little," he went on. "You see, they knew I had money, and was willing to spend it—you can't blame them, Miss Marvin; they were a poverty-stricken lot! It's no wonder that the prospect of a square meal and a little recreation tempted them."

"No, I do not blame them," said Faith, very decidedly; "but I do blame you, Mr. Denton; it was wicked of you to tempt them."

The young man's face fell, and he shifted his position uneasily.

"We can't all be sincere," he said, rather irritably, "and what seems right to one often seems wrong to another. I've been careless, I admit, and perhaps a little wicked, but don't condemn me utterly, Miss Marvin. Why not try to reform me?"

Faith glanced at him sharply. There was not a trace of mirth in his face. It was evident that he had asked the question in earnest.

"I wish I could," she answered, smiling a little; "but if you really wish to reform, you can do it yourself, Mr. Denton. You have only to pray, and your God will aid you."

"But I lack faith," he said, quickly. "I don't see things as you do, and, besides, 'the prayers of the wicked are an abomination unto the Lord;' you see, I know that much about the Bible, Miss Marvin!"

"But you will be wicked no longer when you go to Him in the right spirit," said Faith, brightly. "Oh, go to Him, Mr. Denton. It will give such pleasure to your father!"

"I'm afraid I can't," said young Denton, rising. "I have one of those natures that cannot accept the marvelous, and, further, I'm too great a sinner to reform, I guess; but please don't forget me because of that, Miss Marvin. I would give more than I can tell to have you think well of me."

Again the admiring glance rested upon the fair girl's face, and it took all Faith's composure to reply sedately.

"I shall be glad to think well of you," she said, a little shyly; "but you have much to undo, I'm afraid, before that can be accomplished."

"You are thinking now of what you have heard of me," said the young man, quickly.

"I am thinking of what I have seen," was Faith's decided answer, "and I cannot think well of you when I look at poor Maggie Brady."

"Don't mention her name!" cried her caller, almost angrily. "It is bad. enough for you to have to work with her, but it is worse to know that you are wasting your thoughts on her!"

"Mr. Denton, I am ashamed of you!" Faith's voice rose instinctively. "How dare you speak disrespectfully of one of your own victims?"

A half sneer passed over the young man's face.

"I thought she'd been telling a lot of tales," he said, fiercely. "No doubt she has blackened my character through and through! I can never hope to overcome your impression of me, Miss Marvin!"

"On the contrary!" said Faith, hotly, "she has never spoken of you to me! All that she ever said of you was said on those two occasions in your presence. But she doesn't have to speak, for I can see it in her face. That girl's soul is on your conscience. You are responsible for her, Mr. Denton!"

Young Denton turned and looked at her searchingly.

"So long as you believe that, there is no hope for me," he muttered.

The next moment he bowed silently and left the apartment. When he had gone Faith stood a moment almost trembling with excitement. She did not even try to explain her many conflicting emotions. This much she knew—she pitied him exceedingly, he was so young, so weak—she could reason no further.

When her mother came in she was crying softly. The events of the day had completely unnerved her.

Mrs. Marvin finally succeeded in comforting her a little, and then followed plans for the future, both for themselves and others.

They decided to move as soon as possible, so that they could accommodate little Dick in a more satisfactory manner, and also have a room for a servant and one for visitors.

It was a pleasant programme, and its arrangement cheered Mrs. Marvin wonderfully. She was one of those women who droop under adversity, but who spring up like a flower at the first gleam of sunshine.

Contrary to her wishes, Faith insisted on going to the store the next morning. She was so decided about the matter that Mrs. Marvin dared not argue.

"I shall say nothing about our fortune," she said, as she started, "until I see exactly how it will affect my position as a helper."

The new cloak-room was swarming with girls when she arrived, and as soon as Lou Willis saw her she shouted to her:

"Hello! Miss Marvin! have you heard the news? Lightning has struck downstairs, and it is raining surprises!"

"It's a pity lightning didn't strike the jewelry counter," called another voice; "but if it did, I suppose it would find Lou insulated! You'd go on talking just the same; ain't that so, Willis?"

"I talk when I have anything to say," was the girl's curt answer, "but at present, if you please, I am addressing Miss Marvin!"

"Dear me, how respectful we are to some folks!" was the mocking reply. "How did you manage, Lou, to get that handle before the Marvin?"

"Oh, do shut up!" was Lou's emphatic reply. "I want to tell my news and you are not giving me the chance! They say that old Forbes has gone home sick! He can't stand the racket!"

"What do you mean?" asked Faith, as she hung up her hat.

"Why, the boss' religious attack has upset him completely—knocked him out in one round—and I don't much wonder. How on earth could you expect any sane man to look on at the changes in this store and not shake in his shoes if he has money invested in the business?"

"What has Mr. Denton done now?" asked Faith, with great interest.

"Hired a lot of new hands, for one thing," was Lou's prompt answer, "and raised the salaries of more than half the clerks in the building!"

"Is that so, really?" asked a dozen voices.

"Well, as this happens to be my truthful day, you can depend upon it," said Miss Willis, laughing. "Oh, I tell you, girls, the millennium is coming! I expect he'll provide us soon with private carriages to ride to business!"

"Well, he has one of his own," remarked Miss Jones, from the distance. "He might at least hire a stage for us in stormy weather."

"An excellent idea!" exclaimed Faith, impulsively; "only, as we live so far apart and there are so many of us, I'm afraid the suggestion is a little impracticable."

"Then let him provide a dozen," cried another girl, laughing. "What is the cost of a dozen stages to a concern worth millions?"

"Oh, girls!" cried cash girl Number 83, as she came bounding in, "what do you think has happened? Mag Brady has been arrested! They say she's been trying to poison Miss Marvin!"

Faith sank down in a heap on one of the new sofas which Mr. Denton had lately provided for their comfort.

It was out at last, in spite of their caution. For a moment she was stunned by the suddenness of it.

The clerks all clustered around her and began asking questions, but she was too dazed to even think of answering any of them.

"I knew she'd do it!" cried Lou Willis, exultantly. "I've warned you against her a dozen times, Miss Marvin, but that's what you get for riling a jealous woman!"

"She'll have a chance to get over her jealousy now," said Miss Jones. "If they can prove that on her they'll send her to prison!"

Faith staggered to her feet and faced them resolutely.

"They shall never prove it, if I can help it," she said, finally, "for I am sorry for Miss Brady, and I'm going to try and save her!"

CHAPTER XXXII
ANOTHER TALK WITH THE INSPECTOR

As Faith rushed from the cloak-room she came suddenly upon Ben Tyler, who was standing at the head of the stairs leading down into the private offices.

"Oh, Mr. Tyler, do please tell me about poor Miss Brady!" she cried, eagerly. "I have only just heard that she has been arrested!"

The detective smiled grimly at the eagerness in her manner, but he was nothing loath to relate his prowess.

"She's arrested all right! I nabbed her last night," he said, promptly, "but she had covered her tracks pretty well. I had a deuce of a time to prove it!"

Faith was still staring at him speechlessly, but with questioning eyes. She could not help feeling some curiosity about the details of the story.

"First, I had to find the boy that brought the candy to the store," went on the detective; "then I traced it step by step until I reached Mag Brady. Her brother is in a drug-store; it was through him she got the poison."

"And where is she now?" asked Faith, beginning to tremble.

"In jail, where she belongs!" was the heartless answer. "Mr. Denton and I went to court this morning and had her locked up for safe keeping."

"Oh, I didn't think he would do it!" said Faith, almost ready to cry. "It is cruel, Mr. Tyler! Oh, I am so sorry for Miss Brady!"

"Well, I wouldn't be sorry for a person who tried to kill me," said the detective, sneeringly; "but, then, I'm no saint like you, Miss Marvin."

Faith looked at him quickly and could see a sneer on his face. It was plain that he had no special respect for saintliness.

When she reached her department she found every one talking excitedly, and, of course, Miss Brady's arrest was the topic of conversation.

"Here she comes!—here comes Mag's rival!" cried Miss Jones, when she saw Faith coming.

The "head of stock" had got down before her and was beginning to arrange her goods upon the counter.

"So she tried to kill you, did she?" asked Miss Fairbanks, coming up. "Well, all I've got to say is, the Lord deliver me from any dealings with a jealous woman!"

Faith set her lips firmly and did not speak. She was determined to shield Maggie in every way possible.

"I thought your habits would lead you into trouble, Miss Marvin," said Mr. Gunning, insolently. He was leaning over the counter, which was as near as he could get to her. Still Faith did not answer, but went on with her work. There were no customers in yet, so she had no haven of refuge to fly to.

"How's the mash with the nigger servant?" asked Miss Jones, suddenly. "Has he got a wife, Miss Marvin? You'd better look out if he has! You know Mag Brady isn't the only jealous woman in creation!"

Faith looked at her steadily before she answered, and for a second the treacherous eyes wavered and Miss Jones felt decidedly uncomfortable.

"Neither Miss Brady nor any other woman has cause to be jealous of me," said Faith, plainly. "I have never wronged any human being, and I cannot understand, Miss Jones, why you insist upon taunting me!"

"Oh, don't mind her, Miss Marvin, she can't help it," cried Miss Fairbanks. "She's been crossed in love, and it makes her spiteful!"

There was a shout from every girl that had heard the buyer's words, and for once the tables were turned upon Faith's tormentor.

At about ten o'clock several new clerks entered the department, Miss Fairbanks assigning them places and giving them their instructions.

"Now one of you girls can go to the cloak-room and rest for twenty minutes," she said to Miss Jones and Faith. "It's Mr. Denton's orders that you are not to be on your feet so steadily."

"You go first," said Faith, turning to Miss Jones, pleasantly.

The woman blushed a little and left the counter sullenly.

"Miss Fairbanks!" called Faith, as soon as she had disposed of several customers, "please come over here a minute; I want to speak to you!"

Miss Fairbanks came over and stood close by the counter. She felt sure that Faith was about to confide about Miss Brady.

"Miss Fairbanks, I want you to help me," the young girl whispered. "I want you to help me get better acquainted with Miss Brady, and, if possible, show me a way to win her confidence."

"For mercy's sake, what for?" asked the buyer, in amazement.

"Simply to give me a chance to prove my innocence, for one thing; I want her to know that I never even had the desire to see Mr. James Denton, much less to flirt with him!"

"Is that true?" asked the buyer, gazing at Faith very seriously.

The color mounted swiftly to the cheeks and brow of the young girl, but, without turning her eyes, she answered:

"It is quite true, Miss Fairbanks."

"That would mean that we'd have to go to jail to see her," said the buyer, slowly, "and I confess I'm not in love with that sort of visiting."

"But surely it won't harm us," urged Faith, very eagerly. "You go first, Miss Fairbanks, and tell her that I wish to see her; if I should go first, I'm afraid she wouldn't see me."

"Very well, I'll do it," said Miss Fairbanks, after a minute. "I'm sorry for the girl, and I'm not ashamed to admit it."

"Oh, thank you, Miss Fairbanks, and do try to make her see me!" cried Faith. "I'm sure we can do some good, even if it is only by showing her that we love her."

"My goodness! You don't love her, do you, Miss Marvin? Why, from all accounts the girl intended to kill you!"

"Nevertheless, I love her—in a way," said Faith. "I can't forget entirely that she is only an erring sister."

"Well, you are a good girl, if ever there lived one," said Miss Fairbanks. "You are teaching me a whole lot about practical Christianity."

"Goodness, that which is not practical—is poor stuff," said Faith, bitterly. "I wouldn't be a hypocrite for all the world, and that is exactly what sham goodness amounts to; still, I don't mean to say, Miss Fairbanks, that I've always lived up to what I knew was my duty! I've made lots of mistakes, but I was always sorry!"

She sighed a little as she turned away, but her sadness soon changed to smiles as she saw Miss Dean standing beside her counter.

"How do you do, Miss Marvin?" asked the lady inspector, cordially. "I am delighted to see you again, for I was afraid I was never going to!

Business is so very brisk," she said, laughingly, as she saw Faith's questioning expression. "Why, I'm up to my ears in modern improvements! I'm a carpenter, an engineer and a full-fledged plumber!"

"Do you have to know a lot about all such things?" asked Faith.

"Well, not a lot, exactly, but just enough. We have to know when stores are lacking in either of the things mentioned."

"There have been many changes since you were here," said Faith, slyly. "We have a new cloak-room now; you just ought to see it!"

"Oh, I have seen it, you can be sure!" said the lady, dryly. "I've been up there sniffing around and inspecting every corner, and I'm glad to say that I quite approve of it."

They both laughed heartily, but Faith was not quite satisfied.

"Can you see any changes that you did not suggest. Miss Dean?" she asked, a little timidly. "Are there no improvements that look to you like radical reforms, suggested by the divine spirit of love for humanity?"

"Not one!" said Miss Dean, promptly. "I see nothing of the sort! There are no changes here that could not have been effected by the law of common decency! I should feel sorry to think that a man could not do what was right without a divine suggestion. It would speak ill of his sense of honor or justice toward humanity."

She paused a moment and then began speaking more slowly. There was no resentment in her tones; she was merely reasoning the situation.

"I can see that the firm of Denton, Day & Co. has come to a crisis in its business career, owing to the illogical stand recently taken by one of its members. From a paying investment it has turned into a philanthropical institution, and so long as it can live as such it will be a great benefit to hundreds. Further than this, I hear that one man has made an unjust fortune by withdrawing from the firm and that another partner is watching like an eagle for an opportunity to swoop down and settle his talons. Then, again, I understand from a reliable source that Mr. Denton's wife is fast going insane from worry, and that his scapegrace son is growing gray-headed over the outlook for his fortune. Again, Mr. Denton himself, who has wrought all these changes, is being looked upon by wise men as a driveling idiot, or, what is about as bad, a religious fanatic, whose sudden determination to be good has sealed the doom of his fortune."

As Miss Dean was speaking she looked steadily at Faith. She was watching to see if her words had any effect, or if the girl was really incapable of understanding the situation.

There was not a cloud of apprehension upon the fair girl's brow, yet her eye was clear; she had comprehended every syllable.

"You approve of all this?" asked Miss Dean, in despair.

Faith's answer was merely a verse of Scripture, which she repeated so firmly and with such intense eagerness that the low voice fairly vibrated with repressed emotion.

"And be ye not conformed to this world; but be ye transformed by the renewing of your souls, that ye may prove what is that good and acceptable and perfect will of God."

"I am answered, as I fully expected to be," said Miss Dean, quietly. "It is positively wonderful, that faith of yours. Why, it amounts to actual exaltation of spirit!"

She shook hands with Faith and said good-by. They were the extremes of goodness, accomplishing the same ends, but each working on a theory incomprehensible to the other.

CHAPTER XXXIII
FAITH VISITS MAGGIE

The next few days were busy ones for Faith, for, besides her work at the store, she helped pack every evening, and tried in every way possible to enter into the spirit of the new arrangements for living, which her mother was planning so enthusiastically.

At last they were settled in a handsome flat in a neighborhood where Faith was not afraid to let either little Dick or her mother go out alone, and this one fact made her very happy.

Not a word had escaped her at the store about her altered conditions, neither had she spoken again to her mother regarding her uncle.

Mrs. Marvin told her sadly that he had gone abroad immediately after arranging the transfer of the $50,000 and settling all the details of her newly acquired fortune. Faith breathed a sigh of relief, although she felt sorry for her mother. It was evident that his humiliation was deep and genuine.

She frequently caught herself wondering about his changed name. He was born a Courtleigh, yet he had signed himself "Deering."

She decided at last that it was a purely personal matter. Doubtless it was for some reason which she in her innocence would neither understand nor approve.

Other things which she could understand were claiming her attention, so that there was little time to spend in idle conjectures.

She waited eagerly as the days passed by for a word from Maggie Brady that she was willing to see her.

At last it came, and Faith hurried down to the jail. She had no difficulty whatever in securing Mr. Denton's permission.

At the first glimpse of Maggie behind prison bars she nearly burst into a fit of crying. The girl was so haggard and pale that she hardly knew her.

"I suppose you've come to gloat over me," were the prisoner's first words, "but it don't matter to me. You can come if you want to."

"Oh, Miss Brady, don't say that," cried Faith, with the tears springing to her eyes. "I have come to see you—to try and cheer you. Do, please, believe me!"

"How do you expect to cheer me?" asked Maggie sullenly, as the keeper opened the door of her cell and let her out into the corridor.

"I don't know that I can," said Faith, very sadly, "but you will let me try, at least, won't you, Maggie?"

There was a yearning in her voice that the woman could not miss. She stared at Faith steadily, as though trying to read her soul, and in a moment her face softened and she spoke more gently.

"Oh, I have no doubt you are sorry for me, and all that," she said slowly. "That's natural, but, see here; I don't want any sympathy."

"But you do want my friendship, don't you, Maggie?" said Faith; "and that is what I have come to offer you—just my honest friendship."

In an instant the fiend in the girl woke again.

"Do you expect me to believe that?" she hissed in a whisper, "after doing your best to cut me out with Jim Denton?"

She glanced at the girl with a perfect storm of fury in her eyes, but Faith's glance did not waver; she only shook her head sadly.

"I am sorry you will not believe me, Maggie," she said softly, "but it is the truth that I have never flirted with Mr. Denton, and the only times I ever saw him in my life before this trouble arose were twice, when you saw us together."

"I don't believe you," said her listener, sharply. "If you had never flirted with him why did he send you candy?"

"I don't know, I am sure," said Faith hopelessly. "Perhaps he thought I was young and silly, and would not know that he was insulting me."

Miss Brady looked at her with some surprise in her eyes.

"Did you consider it an insult?" she asked, slowly.

"Certainly," said Faith. "He had no right to do so. He forced it upon me; I did not want it."

"And he has never made love to you?" asked the woman eagerly.

She was bending forward, staring at Faith with a strained expression upon her features. To save her life, Faith could not help blushing. Hers was a tell-tale face—it portrayed every emotion.

"I knew it! I knew it!" cried Miss Brady sharply. "You would not blush as you are doing if he hadn't done it!"

"But he hasn't, I assure you," said Faith, as soon as she could speak. "Mr. Denton has flattered me a little, of course, but I can honestly say that he hasn't made love to me."

She was firm enough now, and her voice was very convincing. Miss Brady gazed at her steadily and seemed impressed with her candor.

"Well, he hadn't better," she muttered sullenly. "Jim Denton had better take care—" She stopped suddenly. "I had forgotten," she said bitterly; "I am helpless and in prison."

"But I am sure you will soon be free, Miss Brady," said Faith, "for I have utterly refused to appear against you, and—"

"What!" exclaimed the woman in a startled whisper. "You have refused to appear against me—and you think me guilty?"

"If I knew you were guilty I would still refuse," said Faith stoutly, "for if you sent that candy you must have been crazy!"

Slowly the frown lifted from the poor girl's brow. She kept gazing at Faith as though she could hardly credit her senses.

"You will not accuse me," she stammered again. "Well, that's more mercy than I ever expected on earth or in heaven."

"What is more, Maggie," continued Faith, "I want you to be my friend. As soon as you are out of this place we can see more of each other."

This was a little too much for even Maggie Brady's nature. Her lips trembled suspiciously before she answered.

"Oh, I won't get out; you mark my words. Old Denton will send me up, or, if he don't, the District Attorney will do it."

"I don't think so," said Faith. "They won't if I can prevent it, and as I am the person most interested, I think I should have some voice in the matter."

"You understand, I don't admit that I did it, yet," said Miss Brady, sullenly. "I have never admitted a thing, not even to the lawyer."

"Would you not be happier if you did admit it?" asked Faith, softly. "I am sure it would relieve you to get it off of your conscience."

"Oh, it ain't troubling me much!" said the girl indifferently, "but I will say that I'm glad the stuff didn't kill you!"

"But it might have killed Sam Watkins if the dog had not happened to be there. Why, Miss Brady, just think; you might have killed a dozen people!"

The woman shuddered and turned away her face.

"Well, as it didn't kill any one there's some hope for me," she said, "and I want to live long enough to get square with Jim Denton!"

"What has he done to you?" cried Faith, impulsively. "I can't think what he could do to make you hate him so bitterly."

"Hate him!" cried the girl. "Me hate Jim Denton! Why, you don't know what you are talking about! Would I be jealous if I hated him?"

"But you certainly can't love him," said Faith, with another blush. "If you did you could not harm him so much as in your thoughts. You would be glad to suffer anything to be able to protect him."

"Oh, I've protected him all right," said the girl, with a sneer; then she straightened up suddenly and said:

"I want to ask you a favor. I want you to bring old Denton down here," she said eagerly. "Bring him yourself and let Fairbanks come with you. Come any day you like. I'm not particular."

"I will ask Mr. Denton to come, if you wish," said Faith, a little wonderingly, "and I am sure he will come. He is very sorry for you, Maggie."

"He'll be sorrier, I'm thinking," was the answer. "But my time is up. Good-by, Miss Marvin."

"Good-by," said Faith, sweetly, "and you believe me, Miss Brady. You know now that I am innocent in regard to young Mr. Denton?"

"Bring the old man down, and I'll believe it," was her answer. "If you will do that for me, I shall have some faith in your friendship."

When Faith got back to the store she went straight to Mr. Denton, and repeated in as few words as possible her conversation with Maggie.

Mr. Denton had found out himself many things about his son, so Faith did not hesitate to tell the entire story.

"I can't think that my son has really wronged the woman," he said, sadly, "but he has been very reckless, I fear, and it is my fault in great measure."

"And you will go to see her, will you not?" asked Faith, eagerly.

"With pleasure," said Mr. Denton, "and I trust that with our words and our prayers, Miss Marvin, that we shall be able to bring the poor sinner to repentance."

Faith left the private office feeling very hopeful and happy. She was more so when she met Mr. Watkins just entering the building.

There was a hearty hand-clasp and an earnest greeting; then Mr. Watkins told her briefly of his recovery and his prospects for the future.

"I am to have the same position; only a much larger salary," he said, brightly, "which will enable us to live in comfort without Sam's working. He can go to day school for at least another year."

"Everything is shining with hope down here," was Faith's answer. "Really, Mr. Watkins, you will be astonished at the changes."

As briefly as possible she told him of her own good fortune, and giving him her new address, she cautioned him to keep it secret for the present.

"And now I have some news that will astonish you," said Mr. Watkins. "A rich old lady, whom I once met, wrote me a letter the other day—she knew my poor sweetheart, and wants to adopt her brother."

"Adopt little Dick?" cried Faith, in distress. "I can hardly think of it, Mr. Watkins; yet we must look into it, of course. I must not let my love for him stand in the way of his welfare."

"That is what I thought," said Mr. Watkins, soberly; "but do you chance to know her, Miss Marvin? Her name is Mrs. Graham."

"Yes, indeed, she's the sweetest old lady in the world," cried Faith. "She used to come in here and shop, and Mary and I both loved her."

"Well, I'm to see her to-night, and hear what she has to say. I will tell you all about it later," he said as they parted.

"It will be a better home than we can give him," murmured Faith, thoughtfully; "for while we have a few thousands, Mrs. Graham has millions."

CHAPTER XXXIV
MR. FORBES REACHES A DECISION

Early the next morning Mr. Denton was in his office. He was almost the first person at the store nowadays, and, as far as he could, he looked after every detail of business.

At half-past eight the sample room was thronged with drummers, and each buyer was carefully inspecting the goods which he intended ordering for his special department.

More than once Mr. Denton interrupted some low conversation where he felt sure that a deal was being made which could not be adjusted to his newly awakened conscience.

Then came the opening of the morning mail. He had always intrusted this to others; now he gave it personal supervision.

Quite frequently he intercepted letters that he did not understand until he had investigated closely, with the aid of a detective, but in each instance the wrong-doer was treated with mercy, he was reasoned with and cautioned, a repetition would mean discharge on the instant.

Thus, almost daily he found fresh evidences of dishonesty, either in the firm's dealing with manufacturers or customers, or some treachery of employees, whose opportunity came to them in the form of mail orders.

Goods were ordered in this way frequently which could not be supplied, and an inferior grade was almost invariably substituted. When this was done the "mail order clerk's" methods were simple—either he or the firm were profiters through the transaction.

Mr. Denton finally thought out the solution of this unpleasant matter, and on this particular morning he summoned the advertising manager for the firm to his office.

Picking up a daily paper, he pointed to one of their attractive "ads."

"Bring me a sample of these goods, Green," he said, a little sternly; "you can get them of Billings, the buyer in that department."

"Oh, that's only a blind, sir," was the startling answer, "Mr. Billings has some old goods that he is trying to work off. They are not quite up to the mark, but that 'ad' will sell them."

"Do you mean by that, Green, that we are misrepresenting our goods?" asked Mr. Denton; "or, in other words, that we are advertising one grade of goods and selling another?"

"That's about it," said the manager, looking a little puzzled, "but it's nothing new, sir; we've always done it!"

Mr. Denton looked at him for a moment before he spoke. He could not censure him for what they had "always" done, neither could he blame the man for his own previous indifference on the subject.

"Don't do it again, Green," he said very sadly, "and send Mr. Billings to me the minute you see him."

As Mr. Green went out Mr. Denton groaned aloud: "Would he ever get to the end of his own dishonesty, or was he to be confronted daily by such contemptible trickery?"

Just once he tried to justify his past methods, but with a sneer of scorn he put such thoughts from him.

As he sat in deep meditation the door opened again. He looked up, and saw that it was Mr. Forbes who had entered.

"I am glad to see you," said Mr. Denton, quickly, "and I hope you are feeling entirely recovered."

Mr. Forbes bowed slightly, as he dropped into a chair.

"Mr. Forbes," said Mr. Denton, "I am ashamed of myself! I never knew until to-day that I was such a scoundrel!"

He pointed to the paper that he still held in his hand, and in a very few words repeated his late conversation.

"That is necessary in business," said Mr. Forbes shortly, "and it is, to say the least, peculiar that you shouldn't know it!"

"Well, it's an infamous trick!" was Mr. Denton's rejoinder. "Just think of the poor people whom we have defrauded in that manner!"

"I prefer to think of the dollars it has brought into our pockets," said Mr. Forbes sullenly, "and now that we are on the subject, I may as well say, Mr. Denton, that I am sick and tired of this whole idiotic business!"

"Do you wish to sell out?"

Mr. Denton spoke calmly. "If so, name your price while I have the money to pay you."

"Oh, you do expect to fail, then? You still have sense enough for that!" said Mr. Forbes quickly. "Then, why not give up your fad at once and run the business properly?"

"Do you mean as we have been running it?" asked Mr. Denton, with a sharp glance at him.

"Certainly, with a few modifications, perhaps," was the equally sharp answer.

"Never!"

Mr. Denton's voice rang out like the blast of a trumpet.

"Go back to such infamous practices? Never!"

"Very well, then," said Mr. Forbes, with sudden anger in his voice, "I do wish to sell out! What will you give me for my interest?"

Mr. Denton wheeled around, and looked at him eagerly.

"I had hoped you would see things differently," he said at last. "I thought that perhaps you would appreciate my desire, which is to make myself more worthy of the God that made me."

Mr. Forbes shifted uneasily, and finally rose from his chair. He was plainly disturbed over the situation.

"I do appreciate your efforts, and I honor them, in a way," he said slowly, "but I have not the courage to make such a sacrifice myself, and I very much doubt if such a sacrifice is demanded. A proper observance of religion is enough; a man need not crucify his worldly ambitions in order to be worthy of heaven."

"'Let him take up his cross and follow Me,'" quoted Mr. Denton. "My cross is to do exactly as I am doing. It is not easy to bear, but I am happy in bearing it."

"But where will it lead to?" asked Mr. Forbes eagerly. "What proof have you that your reward will come? This may be a delusion that you are following."

"I am willing to risk it," said Mr. Denton, solemnly. "It is the best a man can do to follow his conscience."

"But there are duties to one's family that must be considered," urged Mr. Forbes. "A man cannot rightfully ignore the fact that he is of the earth, earthy, and that there is something tangible needed before we soar into the mysteries."

"He must ignore nothing," said Mr. Denton, gravely, "but, as I said before, he must follow his conscience."

"Well, I should like to stay with you, but I cannot do it," said Mr. Forbes, "for, while I sympathize with your feelings in many respects, yet I cannot indorse your unbusiness-like actions. If you think my interest here is worth fifty thousand dollars, you can give me that amount, and I will go—then you will be free to spend your fortune according to any freak of your fancy."

"You are more just in your dealings than I expected," said Mr. Denton, flushing a little. "After my experience with Mr. Day, I did not look for any mercy."

"Oh, I have a conscience, too," said Mr. Forbes, grimly, "and while I did not know it until lately, it has made me very uncomfortable, I can assure you."

There was a genuine ring in his voice as he spoke, and as Mr. Denton detected it, he rose and placed his hand upon his shoulder.

"Better stay with me, brother, and let us work together," he said gently. "In the vineyard of the Master there can be no unrewarded labor."

Mr. Forbes shook his head and turned away.

"We can attend to the legal details some other time," he said briefly. "You are busy to-day, so I will not detain you."

Mr. Denton sat down at his desk again, and as the door closed behind his partner he bowed his head upon his bosom.

"Alone and yet not alone," he whispered softly. "God grant me strength to do my duty, and if my lot is failure, let me accept it bravely. It is all a man can do. He must follow his conscience."

The door opened again, and Faith Marvin entered. She had her hat on, and was ready for the visit to Maggie Brady.

"I wonder what she wishes to see me for?" said her employer, musingly. "Is she desirous of upbraiding me, do you think, Miss Marvin?"

"Why should she upbraid you?" asked Faith, very soberly. "You certainly are not to blame for the actions of your son, and as for her arrest, you simply had to do it."

"She may say that I should have protected her from him," he answered. "Some way I blame myself continually in that particular direction."

"A girl should be able to protect herself," said Faith sternly. "I can't quite understand such weakness in women, unless it is, as poor Miss

Jennings used to say, 'the iniquities of the fathers visited upon generations of the innocent.'"

"I believe that fully," said Mr. Denton with a sigh. "It is one reason why I am merciful in my own boy's case—my sins have been perpetuated! Can I ever efface them?"

They left the building together, going out of one of the side doors. Just as they reached the sidewalk a handsome carriage drew up before the entrance.

"Why, that is my own carriage!" exclaimed Mr. Denton quickly.

The next instant James Denton sprang from the carriage and came face to face with Faith and his father.

CHAPTER XXXV
MAGGIE BRADY'S SECRET

"What is it? Is anything wrong?" asked Mr. Denton quickly.

"Mother is worse," was the short answer. "She's gone out of her head completely."

Mr. Denton paused and rubbed his brow perplexedly.

"Oh, what is it, sir?" asked Faith eagerly. "Is your wife really ill? I have heard it rumored that she was, but I did not know whether to believe it."

"She is, indeed!" exclaimed young Denton, looking angrily at his father; "and she has every reason to be. It is only natural."

"Hush!" exclaimed Mr. Denton sternly. "You shall not criticise my actions. As your father, I expect and demand your silence. I am responsible to God alone—not to my wife or family."

"Well, you will have her to answer for, just the same," said the son, sullenly. "She can't see you throwing away your money and keep her senses much longer."

"For shame!" cried Faith hotly. "Can't you see, Mr. Denton, that your father is sorely distressed? How dare you trample upon his feelings in such a brutal manner?"

James Denton wheeled around and faced the speaker.

"My mother is going crazy," he said, almost gently. "You must pardon me, Miss Marvin, but I love my mother."

Mr. Denton opened the carriage door and motioned for Faith to enter. There was a look in his face that permitted no misunderstanding.

"Your mother's doctor and nurse are with her, are they not? Then I shall not be needed for an hour, and I have an important engagement. I am going to call upon Maggie Brady, one of my son's unfortunate victims," he added slowly.

James Denton turned as pale as death as he listened to these words. For a moment it looked as if he were about to spring forward and drag his father from the carriage in order to prevent this visit. In a second they were rattling away from the door. Faith's last glance showed the young man still standing motionless and livid.

"He fears something from the interview," was her first quick thought. She glanced up at Mr. Denton. It was plainly to be seen by his face that he shared her suspicions.

They were admitted at once to the corridor of the jail, and the keeper allowed Miss Brady to join them.

"How are you to-day, Maggie?" asked Faith as sweetly as she could. "You see, I have kept my promise. I have brought Mr. Denton to see you."

"My poor child!" said Mr. Denton, offering Miss Brady his hand. "I am more than sorry to have been the means of bringing you here; but I had no alternative. I had to do my duty."

"Oh, I don't lay it up against you," said the girl, almost coldly. She had drawn away from him quickly and put her hands behind her. "I suppose you thought I was a dangerous person to be at large—well, perhaps you were right; there's no telling what a jealous woman will do. Did they tell you, Mr. Denton, that I was jealous of Miss Marvin?"

There was a steely ring to her tones as she said the words, and the glance of her eyes was both cold and cruel.

"I heard that it was on account of my son," was Mr. Denton's sad answer. "I am very sorry indeed, Miss Brady, if James ever deceived you."

"Oh, he hasn't deceived me a bit," said the girl quickly. "On the contrary, he took pains to parade his attentions before me."

She laughed a harsh, grating laugh as she answered. Mr. Denton looked puzzled. He could not understand her.

"But perhaps you expected too much from his attentions," said Mr. Denton gently. "Young men are often unscrupulous and say more than they mean to young women. Perhaps he led you to believe that he cared more for you than he did, and in this way gained your affections and did not appreciate them."

"He did all that," said the girl, very coldly; "and I was not the woman to endure such treatment calmly. I'm sorry if I was mistaken in Miss Marvin's part in the matter. She says she was innocent, and I'm willing to believe her."

"Well, what can I do for you?" asked Mr. Denton kindly. "I have already tried to get your case dismissed, and as Miss Marvin refuses to appear against you I think we shall be successful. But if there is anything that James has done—any wrong that I can right, you have only to say so, and I will try to do my duty."

Miss Brady stared at the speaker in undisguised amazement. She could hardly believe that it was Mr. Denton who was speaking. As her employer he had always been cold and distant. She had never looked on him as anything more or less than a despot and tyrant.

"Mr. Denton is perfectly sincere, Maggie," said Faith quickly as she noticed the amazement depicted on her countenance.

"But I don't understand," said the girl, still staring.

"Let me explain," said Faith quickly, "and you must try and believe me, Maggie. Both Mr. Denton and myself are thinking only of your good. We want to help you to see this awful sin which you have committed in the right light—that is, as a sin not only against yourself and your fellow beings, but against the God who made you and who wishes you to love Him."

As she spoke she put her arms around the girl in an affectionate manner. Maggie did not draw away, but remained silent and passive.

"You see, Maggie, you are not wronging any one by your bad temper and your stubbornness as much as you are wronging yourself. These sins always react on one's self, you know. They may hurt and grieve others in some degree, but they sear your own heart with the wounds of agony and shut the light of God's tenderness from your soul. Can you not see it, Maggie, how you have marred your own happiness? Do try, dear, to humble your stubborn spirit? Ask God to help you forgive those who wrong you. Believe me, it will make you far happier than this cowardly revenge."

Faith's tones were so beseeching that Mr. Denton was touched beyond expression. He had never seen a more holy sight than this young girl pleading with tears in her eyes with an erring sister.

"It's easy for you to talk," muttered Maggie finally. "Your life has been different from mine. What do you know of trouble?"

"A great deal," said Faith quickly. "If I did not I could not feel as I do. Why, it is through my own experience that I have come to feel this sympathy for others."

"But you don't understand," said the woman more bitterly. "By 'trouble' I do not mean just hard luck and poverty."

"I think I do understand, Maggie," said Faith, more softly. "And I can still say sincerely that I am very sorry for you. I believe that you have been more sinned against than any of us realize."

"I have, indeed!" cried Miss Brady, sharply. Her lips twitched convulsively and tears trembled on her lashes.

"Then God will surely pity you," cried Faith, almost cheerily. "He will understand the length and breadth of your temptation, Maggie, as well as the injustice which you have suffered."

The poor girl gazed at Faith a moment and then burst out crying.

"Oh, I have been wronged most fearfully," she whispered between her sobs. "And I could not help it. I could bear the agony no longer!"

As she spoke she thrust her hand into the bosom of her dress. In another second she had drawn forth a crumpled paper.

"Read it!" she said hoarsely, holding it out toward Mr. Denton. "Read it, and tell me if you blame me for doing as I did, and after you have read it say again that you will help me!"

With a quick wave of horror coursing through his brain, Mr. Denton took the paper and quickly unfolded it.

Only a glance was needed to show him what it was. Mr. Denton staggered to a chair, his face pale and haggard.

"Oh, what is it?" asked Faith, looking from one to the other.

Maggie Brady gave a short, hoarse laugh as she replied:

"Only the certificate of my marriage to young James Denton!"

CHAPTER XXXVI
JIM DENTON'S CONFESSION

As Maggie Brady made her startling announcement Faith's heart seemed to stop beating. She felt faint and dizzy, and spread out her hands before her as if to ward off something that was fast overcoming her.

She tried to speak, but the words died upon her lips. In another moment she lost consciousness entirely and slipped heavily to the floor of the corridor.

Mr. Denton sprang to his feet and attempted to raise her, while Maggie Brady stood like a statue, with her hands clasped tightly together.

"Poor girl! your news has shocked her," said Mr. Denton absently. "She was over-anxious and excited about your welfare."

"Men are easily deceived," was Maggie Brady's sad answer. "I can explain her condition more reasonably than that—the girl is in love with your son—my husband! I thought so before, now I am absolutely certain!"

One of the jailers came in just then and led Maggie to her cell, and as the door closed behind her Faith came slowly to her senses.

When she had revived completely, Mr. Denton led her quickly from the jail. He was too shocked and grieved himself to wish to remain another moment. During the ride back to the store there was hardly a word spoken in the carriage, for both Mr. Denton and Faith were in the most distressed condition of mind.

In Mr. Denton's mind two thoughts were uppermost, his son's wickedness in the past and his duty in the future. At any other time he would have known how to act, but now he was sorely puzzled. Faith, on the other hand, was hiding her face from almost shame, for she had learned a secret in that brief moment at the jail which was overwhelming her soul in a flood of self-censure.

The fair face of James Denton was constantly before her. His pleading eyes and glances of admiration haunted her. She felt, what she would not own even admit to herself, that in spite of his wickedness she was deeply in love with him.

"It does not seem possible," Mr. Denton said at last. "I know my son was thoughtless, but I did not believe him wicked."

Faith could not speak; she was crying softly. The knowledge of her love had completely crushed her.

"Let me go home, please," she murmured, as her employer helped her from the carriage. "I am afraid I am too nervous to remain at the store."

"Certainly," said Mr. Denton, "and I shall soon follow your example, for if my wife is as ill as my son said, it is my duty to neglect everything and remain at her bedside."

"But has she really lost her reason?" asked Faith, a little timidly.

Mr. Denton sighed heavily before he answered.

"She is worrying unnecessarily to a great extent, I think," he said calmly. "She sees in my new methods and actions only the probable financial results; she cannot see that I am honestly trying to do my duty—to share my large fortune with my fellow-beings."

"But is it not possible to follow your conscience and still prosper?" asked Faith, anxiously.

"That is a question that I cannot answer, Miss Marvin, at this stage of the experiment, but, judging from the present outlook, godliness cannot be profitable from a worldly point of view. But from the spiritual, I am satisfied that it is a success; the consciousness of well-doing is enough for the Christian."

Faith pondered over his words as she hurried home. She was glad that he had awakened a new train of thought, as it enabled her to compose herself from her late excitement.

When she reached her mother's home she found both Mr. Watkins and Mrs. Graham, who had called to get acquainted with little Dick and to tell Mrs. Marvin their plans for his future. It was hard to part with him, but it was clearly for the best. Mrs. Graham could give him advantages that would be impossible to Mrs. Marvin.

This transaction permitted Faith to regain her composure entirely, so that when they were gone she was able to tell her mother all that had happened at the jail.

Mrs. Marvin was shocked and pained at the recital.

"Poor child," she said, sorrowfully, "to think she is really his wife. I wonder what could have been their motive for keeping it a secret!"

Faith shook her head. She did not care to even conjecture. It was a subject that cut her heart like a two-edged sword, for, try as she would, she could not condemn James Denton.

An hour later the maid brought her in a card. Faith could hardly control her feelings as she saw that her caller was no other than young Denton.

"He must have been following me," she said to her mother, "else how did he know that I was not at the store?"

Her mother smiled sadly, but did not answer.

Faith entered the parlor as calmly as she could, but her limbs were trembling and the tears were very near to falling. She knew that she should spurn the coward, whom her whole soul despised, but she could not do it; her strength deserted her.

James Denton rose suddenly as she entered the door. He looked like a ghost—he was so pale and haggard. Before she realized it, Faith extended her hand, then she drew it back quickly with a sudden revulsion.

"No, don't offer to shake hands with me," said James Denton, slowly. "I am not fit to touch the hem of your garment, Miss Marvin."

Faith looked at him as he stood there, pale, hollow-eyed and dejected, then with almost a cry she burst out impulsively:

"Oh, how could you do such a thing, Mr. Denton? How did you dare to wrong that poor girl as you have? Don't you know that in so doing you have branded yourself a coward?"

"So she has told you and saved me from doing so?"

Young Denton breathed a sigh of relief. He had come too late with his awful confession.

"Yes, she told us, your father and me," said Faith, faintly. "Oh, it is dreadful—dreadful; I can't understand it!"

"Neither can I," said James Denton, with a tinge of bitterness in his voice. "I have never understood how I came to do it. I was a fool—an imbecile—a lunatic, Miss Marvin. I married the girl without even dreaming that I loved her."

Faith stared at him in surprise as he spoke the words. She was conscious even of a flutter of happiness as she listened to the confession.

"Then why did you marry her?" she asked at last. She watched eagerly to hear his answer.

"It was all done for a lark," began the young man. "We were out with some friends, Miss Brady and I, and I—I suppose we had all been drinking too much; then some one suggested a wedding, and I was fool enough to play the bridegroom."

"And you did not love her?"

Faith asked the question slowly.

"Not a bit, Miss Marvin; I liked her, of course. But she was in love with me; I discovered that later."

"Why did you not own her as your wife?"

Faith hardly knew her own voice as she asked this. It hardly seemed possible that she could speak so calmly.

Mr. Denton looked at her sharply before he replied.

"You can guess that surely," he said very softly. "Rascal that I was, I was ashamed to own her."

After a minute he went on with almost desperate calmness, as though he was determined to tell the whole of the distressing secret.

"I told her that dad would disown me if he knew that I had married her, but that if she would wait until I was twenty-one, that there would be no more danger of my losing my money. Mag likes money, you know, and she consented readily, but when she saw me flirting with the other girls, as I had to, you see, to make every one think that I was still single, her jealousy got the best of her, and you know what happened."

"Well, you will have to own her now," said Faith in almost a whisper.

She had been praying silently for strength to say it calmly.

"Never!" cried young Denton with a flash of anger in his eyes.

"Own a murderess for my wife—never! never! Miss Marvin!"

"Then I shall despise you," said Faith, with a flush of color in her cheeks. "For it is the only thing you can do to right the wrong that you have done her."

"But I can't. Indeed, I can't!" cried the young man, wildly. "Don't you see, Miss Marvin, that I have nothing to give her, no love, no respect, not even friendship?"

"But you must own her, just the same," said Faith, decidedly. "Maggie was a good girl once; it is love for you that has ruined her."

James Denton was even paler than when he entered as he answered her, and there was a tone in his voice that made Faith shudder.

"Two wrongs cannot make one right, Miss Marvin," he said, firmly, "and to live with Maggie would be as great a wrong as the first, for I cannot do so honorably while I love another."

Faith looked up at him quickly and found his gaze riveted on her face. For a moment she seemed drawn to him as if by a magnet, then the revulsion came again and she raised both hands imploringly.

"Go, go, Mr. Denton!" she cried in a sharp whisper. "Please go before you say what is in your heart, for your words can only add cruel mockery to dishonor!"

CHAPTER XXXVII
THE BLESSING OF REPENTANCE

A week passed before Faith went to the store again. She was too utterly miserable to think of resuming her duties.

Mr. Watkins called on her every night to bring her news of the store, and by this means she kept track of all Mr. Denton's changes.

One night Mr. Watkins had mentioned a number of things which had benefited the clerks as well as the customers, and in concluding his recital he sighed very heavily, an indication to Faith that there was something more behind it.

"Why do you sigh, Mr. Watkins?" she asked, abruptly. "It seems to me that these changes should bring nothing but smiles, they are such necessary reforms, yet they have been so long in coming."

"I was thinking of Mr. Denton, I suppose," was the answer. "He's such a good man now that I hate to see him go to the wall completely. Why, Miss Marvin, have you any idea what these reforms have cost? I cannot tell you the figures exactly, of course; but the bills for the past month are enough to frighten one. If he continues his present methods he will not be in business a year longer."

"I thought so," said Mrs. Marvin, quickly. "Religion and business cannot be combined. The man who follows his conscience is sure to lose money."

"But he gains that which is better," spoke up Faith, quickly. "Ask Mr. Denton if this is not true. He has found it so already."

"Well, his poor wife doesn't share his sentiments," said Mr. Watkins, "for she has worried so fearfully over his enormous losses already that she is now on the verge of losing her reason."

"Poor soul," said Mrs. Marvin; "she must be a very worldly woman, for, while extreme poverty is cruel, still, she will probably never reach that condition."

"I am not so sure," replied Mr. Watkins, "but even moderate comfort would be cruel to her, for she was born and has always lived in the lap of luxury."

"I suppose the news of her son's wickedness has distressed her also," said Mrs. Marvin, slowly.

Faith's cheeks flushed hotly, and she bent her head over her sewing,

"She has tried to get him to have the marriage annulled," was Mr. Watkins' answer. "It could easily be done, as both parties were intoxicated."

"And will not the young man agree?" asked Mrs. Marvin, mildly. "I should think he would be just the kind to jump at the opportunity."

"His father will not hear of it," said Mr. Watkins, "and of late even the young man himself has shown a willingness to own her."

Faith raised her head with a light shining in her eyes.

"Then he is not altogether bad," she said, very quickly. "If he does right to Maggie now we ought all to forgive him."

She spoke so earnestly that, both her mother and Mr. Watkins looked at her sharply.

If her mother understood her eagerness, she did not betray it, but with Mr. Watkins it was different. He understood and was nettled.

"Is Mr. Day in business again?" asked Mrs. Marvin, who seemed suddenly to find it necessary to change the conversation.

"No, he has gone abroad to spend his money," answered Mr. Watkins. "He says that he made a small fortune out of another man's religion, and that is far more than he has ever made out of his own, for that was never known to bring him in a penny."

"That is a dreadful thing to say," replied Mrs. Marvin, slowly, "for, while I do not get much comfort out of my belief in God, still, I realize that, it is my own stubbornness that keeps me from it. Some day I hope to understand it better."

"You certainly will, dear mother," said Faith, brightly, "but if you would only stop trying to understand! If you would only accept it as a little child, and then trust to the Heavenly Father to lead you!"

"I will some day, Faith—I am sure of it," answered her mother. "I shall be saved, not only through my own faith, but through that of my daughter."

"Her trust is sublime," said Mr. Watkins, gently. "I shall never forget how she comforted my poor Mary."

"She comforts every one," said Mrs. Marvin, smiling, "I named her rightly—don't you think so, Mr. Watkins?"

"You did, indeed," said the young man, tenderly. "It will be a lucky man, indeed, who can say 'My Faith,' and by those words indicate your daughter, Mrs. Marvin."

"Oh, don't!" said Faith, laughing. "You are mocking, Mr. Watkins."

Like her mother, she, too, found it convenient to change the subject.

"And how about Mr. Forbes? Have you heard anything of his plans?" she asked, eagerly. "I have heard it rumored that he, too, was trying to follow his conscience."

Mr. Watkins smiled as he answered her question.

"He is trying to do what many men have done before him. He is trying to buy his conscience with the money he makes dishonestly, or, in other words, he is a sinner on week-days and a saint on Sundays. Why, they tell me he has started in business for himself, and with what he can gouge from the just wages of his employees he pays pew rent and gives to the heathen. It is the same old story—hypocrisy and greed! Drain the blood of the poor in order to build monuments to their ashes!"

Mr. Watkins spoke bitterly and with a tightening of the lips.

He was thinking of Miss Jennings as he finished his utterance.

After he had gone Mrs. Marvin spoke suddenly to Faith.

"Do you know, dear," she said, simply, "I believe Mr. Watkins is learning to love you! He is a fine young man. Do you think you could care for him?"

"Oh, no, no, mother! Don't ever speak of such a thing!" cried Faith, as if the suggestion hurt her.

Mrs. Marvin looked at her keenly. Her suspicions were being verified.

The next morning Faith was well enough to report for duty, and the very atmosphere of the store seemed changed as she entered.

Miss Fairbanks greeted her with honest cordiality. There were tears in her eyes as she spoke to Faith of Maggie Brady.

"Poor girl," she whispered; "she feels dreadful about her lot. She wishes she had kept silent forever about being Jim's wife and allowed him to free himself, which he could have done very easily."

"But I thought she loved him," said Faith, faintly.

"So she does," was the answer; "but she knows it was wrong for her to marry as she did. She says she knew he did not love her, and felt sure that he would never own her."

"But he does now," said Faith, with a questioning look at the buyer.

"Yes, I believe he has admitted that she is really his wife, but the poor girl has demanded that the marriage be annulled."

Faith looked up eagerly, but she could not frame her question.

"She has been praying, she tells me," said Miss Fairbanks, continuing, "and she says it is her duty to give Jim up, for to live with him would be wicked when he does not love her."

Faith heard only the first words that Miss Fairbanks had spoken. Poor Maggie had been praying; then her heart was softened.

"She is out, you know, and free as air," continued Miss Fairbanks, "but she is not coming back to the store. Mr. Denton has made her an allowance."

"And you, Miss Fairbanks?" asked Faith, very softly. "Are you praying, too, or is it not yet the Lord's time? I am anxious for you to be happy in the 'light of His countenance.'"

Miss Fairbanks laid her hand upon the young girl's shoulder.

"Thank God," she said devoutly; "at last I am praying."

As Faith moved on toward her counter she saw Miss Jones waiting for her. There was something in the girl's manner that struck Faith as unfamiliar.

"Miss Marvin," she said, the moment Faith stepped behind the counter, "I am a rude, treacherous person, and I have wronged you cruelly! Have you the grace in your heart to forgive a traitor?"

Faith grasped her hand, while the tears sprang to her eyes.

"There is nothing to forgive, dear Miss Jones," she said, gently. "We have been sisters from the first, only you did not understand it; but tell me, is it through Miss Fairbanks that you feel so differently?"

"Partly through her and partly through Mag Brady," was the honest answer. "Mag has told me how you talked to her, and she also told me what her husband said, that it was through your influence that he was now willing to own her."

"Did Mr. Denton say that?" asked Faith, speaking slowly.

"He did," said Miss Jones, promptly, "and Mag just blesses you for it."

If Faith had felt one misgiving over that particular action, it vanished now like a bit of vapor.

Mag "blessed" her for the words that had hurt her so to speak. Surely there was balm for all wounds, even those which burned the deepest.

Faith's morning was the happiest she had ever known in the store and at the luncheon hour, as she went to the cloak-room, she had but one wish in her heart, and that was for the conversion of wicked Lou Willis.

CHAPTER XXXVIII
LOU IS CAUGHT AT LAST

As Faith passed Mr. Denton's office on the way to the cloak-room she heard a woman's voice raised to a very high pitch, and immediately recognized it as belonging to Miss Willis.

She had hardly had time to wonder what had occurred, when the door flew open and she had a good look right straight into the office.

Ben Tyler, the detective, was standing with his hand on the door and a very ugly expression on his face, while a few feet further back stood Mr. Denton, apparently trying to reason with the infuriated woman.

One glance was enough to tell Faith what had happened. Lou had been stealing again, and the detective had caught her.

For a moment the young girl hardly knew what to do, and in that momentary hesitation she heard what Lou was saying.

"He's a sneak and a liar!" she screamed, pointing at the detective. "He can't prove that I stole anything! I defy him to do it!"

"But the goods were found in your pocket," said Mr. Denton, firmly.

"Oh, that doesn't prove anything," was the girl's quick answer. "It's very easy for any one to put stolen goods in my pocket; it's been done before, and both of you know it!"

"But I saw you take the watch," said the detective, angrily. "So what's the use of denying it any longer!"

Faith was hurrying away now as fast as she could go. She knew it was not her place to interfere in such matters.

"A month ago I might have done so," she whispered to herself, "but now that Mr. Denton is a Christian, he will deal mercifully with her."

When she reached the cloak-room the utmost excitement prevailed, and the first words that Faith heard distinctly were spoken by the "head of stock" in the jewelry department.

"I've suspected her for a long time," she said, a little viciously. "She's a good-for-nothing, anyway, who isn't above stealing!"

"They say her father was a thief; so it runs in the family, I guess," said another voice; "and then, her mother was a bad character; so Lou comes by it honestly!"

"Oh, girls! don't!" cried Faith, who could endure it no longer. "Please don't say such cruel things! It is dreadful to bear them!"

"Well, they are true, so why shouldn't we say them?" asked one.

"She's been caught 'dead to rights,' so what's the use of mincing matters?" said another.

"But does it do any good to bring up all these things?" asked Faith. "If the poor girl 'comes honestly by them,' should we not be charitable even in speaking of her?"

"There is something in that," spoke up a woman that Faith did not know, "It's another case of the 'sins of the fathers being visited upon the children.' If there was nothing else in the world to keep me from believing in a God, that verse in the Bible would surely do it!"

"Well, I don't need that verse," said another voice, "for the misery and injustice on earth are enough to prove that no God of love or mercy could possibly have ordained it."

"But don't we make a great deal of the injustice and misery for ourselves?" asked Faith, very soberly; "for instance, hasn't Lou just made a lot of misery for herself? She knew she could not go on stealing forever without being punished."

"She probably couldn't help it," was the hesitating answer. "Perhaps she is a kleptomaniac—you know there are such people."

"Oh, but they are always rich people, who can afford to pay the judge for letting them off easy!" said one of the girls, laughing. "When a poor woman steals she's an out-and-out thief; but when a rich woman steals she's a kleptomaniac."

A laugh followed this explanation, but Faith could not join in it. Her thoughts were too full of the fate which had overtaken Lou, and which she knew was only a natural consequence.

Suddenly there was a scream from the direction of Mr. Denton's office, then another, and another, each more shrill and vibrating.

Without a moment's hesitation every girl in the cloak-room started for the stairs. When they got there they saw a sight that made them pale with horror.

Lou Willis was struggling like a maniac between two officers, who were trying to snap a pair of handcuffs on her wrists.

They were both powerful men, but the girl was resisting them fiercely. She slapped and scratched their faces, all the time shrieking her vituperations.

They finally succeeded in locking the "bracelets" and forcing her into a chair—she was too thoroughly exhausted to hold out much longer.

"Do you mean to say that she isn't crazy?" whispered one of the girls on the stairs.

The tears flowed down Faith's cheeks, but she answered the whisper.

"Poor Lou! Poor Lou! She must be crazy! No woman could act or even feel like that and be in her right senses!"

The door of the office was suddenly closed, and, as Lou was silent now, the girls trooped slowly back to the cloak-room.

"They'll take her away as soon as she's quiet," said one, "and that will mean at least six months on Blackwell's Island."

"She's been there before, I think," spoke up a cash girl. "You know, she was caught stealing in another store, but Denton, Day & Co. didn't know it."

"Did you know it when she came here?"

It was Miss Jones who asked the question. She had come in just in time to hear the last of the conversation.

"Of course I knew it, but what of that? Suppose I was going to prevent the girl from earning her living?"

"But didn't you think she'd be apt to steal again?"

The girl laughed coarsely before she answered.

"Well, to tell you the truth, I hoped she would!" she said, glibly. "I would like to have seen her get away with the whole establishment! What were Denton, Day & Co. doing about that time, I'd like to know? Weren't they robbing the poor devils who made their goods, cheating their customers with inferior garments and exorbitant prices, and last, but not least, weren't they wearing the souls out of our bodies with the system of slavery that they employed in the building? What did I care who cheated them or even who robbed them? Wouldn't they grind me to death just as they did poor Miss Jennings? Of course, if it should happen now I should feel very different; still, I'm a good deal sorrier for Lou than I am for Mr. Denton!"

"We would all feel different now," spoke up Faith very quickly. "We would all scorn to be disloyal to such a good employer as Mr. Denton!"

"He's the best friend we girls ever had," spoke up another clerk. "Why, we are in heaven now, compared with what we were a month ago! Shorter hours, bigger pay, no slave-drivers over us, and, best of all, we are treated like human beings. There is no more of that feeling that we are a lot of cattle!"

"The Lord be praised for all His goodness," said Faith, devoutly, "for what but His mercy has enacted this change? It is a demonstration of His love through His servant, Mr. Denton."

"You are right, Miss Marvin," said Miss Jones, firmly. "There is no power on earth that could have altered these conditions, and I for one am ready and glad to admit it!"

Faith looked at the speaker with beaming eyes. It delighted her to witness her companion's fearless demeanor.

"There they go! Lou and the officers!" cried cash girl Number 83. "They are almost carrying her down the stairs! I wouldn't be in her shoes for a thousand dollars."

"Perhaps she'll repent, like poor Mag Brady," said Miss Jones, thoughtfully. "After Mag's wonderful conversion, I feel that there is hope for all of us."

Faith wiped the tears from her eyes as she saw the last of Lou.

"Though your sins be as scarlet—" She could not finish the verse. The next instant she burst out crying—she was weeping for Lou Willis.

CHAPTER XXXIX
THE PENANCE FOR SIN

Maggie Brady had been free for exactly a week, but the prison pallor had not yet left her features.

Thanks to Mr. Denton, she had a comfortable home and her husband was awaiting for permission to join her.

She had not seen Faith since that day in the jail when she read the girl's carefully guarded secret, but in the few short interviews which she had with her husband she learned that which caused her to bless the young girl fervently.

James Denton told her honestly that he did not love her, but his manner as he said it was gentle, even tender.

He regretted his foolish marriage, both for her sake and his own, still he was ready now to do his whole duty by her, and it was Faith Marvin's words that had taught him that duty.

But Maggie Brady was a greatly changed woman. There were thoughts in her heart which she revealed to no one, but which influenced her every deed and decision. She had gone over and over her wasted life and could find no blame for any one individual, for, looked at from all points, it was conditions that were her enemies, conditions made by the rich in their greed of plunder.

If she had been stronger she might have combatted these conditions, but the uselessness of such a struggle had been demonstrated by so many—she did not have courage or faith in her own ability to conquer.

Like hundreds of poor girls, she had drifted from bad to worse, until that mad marriage to Jim Denton capped the climax of her wickedness.

Now, with her newly awakened understanding she desired to do penance for her sin. It was a part of that old religion which she had long ago discarded.

At the confessional she told her wrongdoing and received absolution so far as it is in the power of God's mediators to absolve one, but to promise to live, uprightly forevermore did not satisfy her soul. She felt the need of further self-abnegation; she must crucify body and spirit to complete the penance.

With the calmness, even exultation, of a martyr she made her preparations. There were wishes to be expressed and letters to be written.

One of these letters reached Faith as she sat with her mother early one evening; the writing so faint and uneven that she could hardly decipher it.

"Oh, mother! mother!" she cried as she perused it. "Quick! get on your hat and come with me! The letter is from Maggie—she is sick—or dying!"

As they hurried from the house Mr. Watkins joined them. In five minutes they were in a carriage driving swiftly toward Maggie's address.

As Faith opened the door leading to Maggie's rooms she came upon a scene that nearly paralyzed her senses.

Poor Maggie was half lying and half sitting upon a couch, her husband supporting her tenderly while Miss Fairbanks stood by administering a cordial. There was another person in the room whom Faith knew at once to be a physician, but she had eyes nor ears for no one but Maggie.

"Oh, you poor, dear child! What has happened?" she asked quickly as she went over and knelt by the side of the poor creature.

"I thought you would come," whispered Maggie faintly. "I wanted to see you, oh, so much! I wanted—to—thank—you!"

She lay back on her pillow with a stifled groan while James Denton wiped her brow—his own the color of ashes.

"You were so good," murmured poor Maggie again as Faith leaned over her. "You taught me, to pray. May the good God bless you."

She closed her eyes and a sigh escaped her lips. In an instant the physician took her wrist between his fingers.

"Gone," he said, softly, "the poor child is at rest. Cheer up, Mr. Denton, your wife is in heaven."

"Thanks to her," whispered James Denton, with a look toward Faith. She was kneeling, convulsed with sorrow, with her mother's arms about her.

No one really knew how the secret leaked out first, for the physician, acting as he thought wise, refrained from telling it openly, but Faith soon learned that Maggie's death was not natural—she had died by her own hand—it was her full and complete penance.

"It is not for us to judge," whispered Mrs. Marvin when she heard it.

"God alone knew her thoughts," was Faith's tearful answer.

When the news reached the store, even Mr. Denton wept. It was the end of a familiar but heart-rending tragedy.

And now it came time for Faith to change her plans—for reasons of her own she felt that she must stay behind the counter no longer.

James Denton had gone abroad, so she put him out of her thoughts as completely as possible; only a vagrant memory now and then showed her the lurking shadow of her girlish passion.

As soon as she could she had a talk with Mr. Denton, whom she found, as usual, busily working in his office.

"See, Miss Marvin," he said almost gayly as Faith entered the door, "here are a dozen letters from Christian people this morning, all congratulating me on the changes in my store! I have been getting a few every day, but this is a splendid showing! Here is one," he added, selecting an envelope, "who even offers to put a large sum of money at my disposal just as soon as I have proven that Christianity is practicable and profitable."

"And can you do this, sir?" asked Faith very eagerly.

A hopeful expression flitted across Mr. Denton's face.

"Mr. Gibson tells me that our business is increasing every day," he answered slowly, "and that the poor people are flocking in to look at our honest bargains, and you see here I have proof that the rich people are watching us."

"Oh, I shall be so glad!—so thankful!" said Faith, with a bright smile. "I was sure you would be rewarded for setting such a noble example! But I have come to ask a favor, Mr. Denton," she added, softly. "I want you to give me another position in your store instead of the one I occupy at present."

Mr. Denton looked at her, and understood at once.

"In other words, you wish to enlarge your field of usefulness, do you not, Miss Marvin? You think you can shed the light more successfully if you have a wider scope of action."

"That is it exactly," was Faith's glad answer; "but please, Mr. Denton, I don't wish any salary."

Mr. Denton glanced up in a little surprise. He had not yet even heard of her change of fortune.

"Yes, I have money enough now to live comfortably," she explained, "and I can even help others, I think, a little. It came to my mother some time ago, a few thousands that were due her from her father's estate, so we are in a position to be helpful without remuneration."

"And you will stay with me still?" asked Mr, Denton, smiling. "You will sacrifice your liberty and your home life to stay here and labor, Miss Marvin?"

"It will be no sacrifice, I can assure you!" cried Faith, brightly, "for I am far happier here than I would be anywhere else, I fancy!"

"Then I appoint you as general inspector of my store," said Mr. Denton, promptly, "and your duties are to consist of daily talks with the clerks and daily hints to me how I can improve their conditions."

"Oh, that will be delightful!" cried Faith, excitedly, "only I will not promise to be a very wise inspector, for I am so young that I am sadly in need of experience."

"'The fear of the Lord is the beginning of wisdom.' I do not tremble for the results," said Mr. Denton, smiling.

Faith went back to the department and told Miss Fairbanks of the new arrangement, and in less than an hour every clerk in the store knew it.

"Just think, she has money and yet she will stay here," said one, "and she is to look after our interests, which is the strangest thing about it!"

"Everything is strange here nowadays," was the thoughtful reply. "Why, I'm sure this is the only store in the world that is run on a Christian basis!"

The next remark was made in a lower tone, as if the speaker was doubtful of her own statements in the matter.

"And do you know," she said, slowly, "the business of the store is actually increasing! I got it straight from the head bookkeeper that Mr. Denton is holding his own splendidly in spite of the fact that every one predicted a sure failure."

"Well, I hope I shall never have to work anywhere else," was the answer. "It would kill me to go back to those old days of slavery and poor salaries!"

As the weeks passed by, even the greatest doubter became convinced that the business of the store was improving. Great crowds came every day to look about, if not to buy, for their curiosity as well as interest was genuine and unbounded.

Many flocked to the store to compare the prices of goods with those of the other emporiums and to draw their own conclusions as to the sincerity of the enterprise.

A high price on an article was often misleading until the manufacturer's side of the question was explained and understood, and so, too, a low price often produced various criticism from those who could not differentiate between just and usurious profit.

But in the main the efforts of the merchant were pretty fairly understood and a perfect flood of congratulations followed the enlightenment.

"My motto is consideration for the manufacturer, justice to myself and honest value to my patrons," said Mr. Denton to all. "If I vary from this, it will be through error, not malice."

One by one the buyers learned their lesson of right dealing, and the counters of the big establishment showed the result of their labors.

They were filled with goods whose first values had not been depreciated and whose sale profits were in proportion to the labor expended in handling them.

As Mr. Gibson had said, poor people had flocked to the store. They were satisfied that, at last, they would get the worth of every penny.

"It's funny to see how suspicious they were of us at first," he said to Faith one day. "Why, they were more doubtful of us than ever, I do believe, and all because we had enrolled under a Christian banner."

"I don't blame them," said Faith slowly, "for have they not good cause to doubt? Has not hypocrisy and deceit always assumed the garb of Christianity? It is the church people who are to blame for it—the insincere ones, I mean—so many of them are content with words alone. When it comes to deeds they are tried and found wanting."

"That is why I have never believed," said Mr. Gibson slowly. "I saw through their shams and thought they were all alike! Why, most people use religion as a regular coat of mail, behind which they commit every sin in the calendar! And others, particularly business people, use it merely as a trade-mark or sign of respectability, and then laugh in their sleeves at the number of dupes they make with it!"

"Well, there's no sham or hypocrisy in Mr. Denton's dealings," cried Faith, brightly, "for no man could enter upon a Christian course with greater sacrifice, both of friends and money."

CHAPTER XL
A GOLDEN OUTLOOK

One year had passed since Maggie Brady's death, and Faith Marvin was nearing her nineteenth birthday.

She was still living with her mother in their pretty little flat and working faithfully at the store with Mr. Denton. The year had brought many changes in that establishment, and there were many new faces in place of the old ones.

Faith talked over these changes as she sat with her mother and Mr. Watkins in one of their social chats after the day's work was over.

"It hardly seems like the same place," she said, happily. "Why, we are just one big family, with Mr. Denton for our father!"

"And Mr. Denton is certainly holding his own financially," said Mr. Watkins, a trifle reluctantly, "while the papers are full of reported failures all around us."

"I am so glad that Mrs. Denton is recovering," said Mrs. Marvin. "I did sympathize with her so during the first few months of her anxiety!"

"We are all glad she is better," said Faith, quickly, "for she comes down to the store often, and she is really very charming. But the greatest changes are in the clerks themselves," she went on, thoughtfully. "They are so courteous, so loyal and so kind to each other. Why, a new girl is welcomed and made one of us at once, and, no matter what her faults may be, we are almost sure to win her over. Of course, we miss the little cash girls, but the tube system is much better, and it did seem so terrible to think of those children being forced to earn their living!"

Mrs. Marvin nodded her head sympathetically and her daughter continued.

"Mr. Gunning is so different that you would hardly know him," she said, "and do you know, Fred, he and Miss Jones are to be married next Tuesday? The dear girl, through God's grace, has had the happiness to redeem him. Then Miss Fairbanks has developed just the kindest and sweetest sort of character! Why, I believe every girl in the department loves her!"

"What do you hear of Lou Willis?" asked her mother after a moment. "That poor girl who was arrested for stealing jewelry."

"She has just come back from serving her sentence," was Faith's answer, "and Mr. Denton is considering whether he had better reinstate her."

"It will be a great risk," said Mr. Watkins, soberly, "for 'what's bred in the bone will come out in the flesh,' unless, of course, the spirit of Christ takes possession of the body."

"We hope it will," said Faith, almost cheerily, "and then Lou has had a fearful experience—she may be different altogether."

"And Miss Dean," suggested Mrs. Marvin, in a reminiscent manner.

Faith laughed a little before she answered. "She finds nothing to do in the store now," she said, "but we still differ a little in our notions and theories."

Mrs. Marvin left the room a few minutes later. Whether it was done for a purpose or not, Faith did not have time to conjecture.

"Faith, dear Faith," whispered Mr. Watkins, quickly, "am I never, never to hear your answer?"

He bent toward her so pleadingly that Faith closed her eyes instinctively. It cut her to the heart to have to witness his sorrow.

"I have loved you so long, so patiently, dear! Can you not give me some hope, even though it is for the far-distant future?"

"I cannot! Oh, I cannot!" murmured Faith in agony. "Oh, I wish I could, Mr. Watkins, but it is impossible! I cannot love you!"

The young man rose without a word and took his hat from the table.

"Good-night, Faith," he said, gently. "Good-night, little sister! Don't worry about me! Some day I will get over it!"

He went silently away without waiting for Mrs. Marvin. Faith breathed a sigh of relief that her sad duty was over.

"You have refused him, Faith!"

Her mother spoke softly. "Poor fellow! I am sorry, but you know your own mind, darling."

They sat down again and Faith took up a book. A peal at the bell made her drop it suddenly.

A few moments later young James Denton entered. He was taller, broader and deeply bronzed by travel.

"At last, I see you again," he whispered softly as soon as Mrs. Marvin had left them together.

"Tell me of your travels," said Faith very quickly. The color had risen to her face and her heart was beating wildly.

"Well, I went all over Europe and the Continent," he said wearily; "but a year is not long enough for a fellow to down a bad reputation! I have come back to find myself in contempt, the same as before, but I have decided that I shall not run away again. I am going to try and live down what I could not run away from."

Faith looked at him questioningly, but did not speak. The young man understood the glance and hurried with his explanation.

"I am going to work in the store with my father now," he said, quietly, "and I am going to put in a small sum of money that has come to me in the past year from a distant relative."

"But are you not afraid you will lose it?" asked Faith, a little shyly. "You know you always had grave doubts as to the financial results of your father's undertaking."

"Well, what if I do?" asked the young man, smiling back at her. "Others have done as much, and I can but follow in their footsteps, and then reformation to be acceptable should not be half-hearted."

There was a light in his eyes that was not to be mistaken. As Faith beheld it she uttered a cry of joy and held out both hands toward him impulsively.

Young Denton gathered both her hands into one of his own, while his other rested lightly upon her shoulder.

"And after I have proven myself worthy may I claim my reward?" he whispered. "May I ask my good angel to share her labors with me and so crown her noble life with the seal of forgiveness?"

"I have nothing to forgive," whispered Faith, blushing deeply. "If Christ has forgiven there is nothing further."

"And you will marry me, Faith, if I prove worthy?" he murmured. "For, oh, I love you, sweetheart, and I cannot live without you!"

"I will marry you—yes," was the girl's low answer, "if at the end of a year you are still in the faith—still carrying the light to the darkest places."

There was just one kiss to seal the compact, but that kiss was a benediction, a holy consummation.

Meanwhile Mr. Denton was still sitting in his chair, although the big building was empty of all but its watchman.

His head was bowed down upon his bosom, as the year just passed spread panorama-like before his vision.

What had he accomplished of his Master's work? He breathed a sigh that it had been so little.

He had tried to put justice in the place of its opposite, to install sweet liberty in the place of oppression. In his dealings with his fellow men he had been fair and equitable, even leaning toward mercy when opportunity offered.

In fact, he had incorporated the Spirit of Righteousness into the Temple of Mammon and molded worldly affairs after the principles of divine teaching.

And what to him had been the results? He smiled with grateful satisfaction as he briefly reviewed them.

There was a trifling shortage as compared with the accounts of previous years, so trifling that it astonished him when he reflected upon the amounts which he had paid his two partners. Beyond this the business of the store had been good and his books showed new accounts recently opened with wealthy persons, which assured him beyond doubt that they indorsed his methods.

Further than this, there were offers of capital from a dozen different sources. The sincere Christians of the city could not have expressed more tangibly their ardent desire to stand shoulder to shoulder with the merchant who had resolved to deal according to his conscience.

The outlook for the future was more than hopeful. He could see no obstacle in the path of his ultimate victory.

There should be no more grinding down in the work-rooms where his goods were made, no undercutting of prices to ruin a brother merchant.

He should be just with others and they must be just with him or he would refuse absolutely to have dealings with them.

Every employee of his establishment should be suitably remunerated, and by this treatment he felt assured that he would receive their ablest service.

Co-operation in his humane work was all that he needed, and here, on his desk and in his books, was ample proof of this assistance. He bowed his head in thanksgiving as he finished his reflections.

"Surely, with God all things are possible," he murmured audibly, and then a thought of his son's conversion and his wife's gradual but sure return to reason with health brought a flow of happiness that irradiated his countenance.

A glimpse of starlit sky was visible through his window and Mr. Denton raised his eyes to it in solemn contemplation.

"Thy ways are not our ways," he whispered humbly, "but though the cross is heavy and hard to bear, Thou wilt give Thy servant a just reward, and the end is peace—peace that passeth understanding."